First published in Los Angeles, California, United States of America in 2014 by BJ DeHut.

ISBN – 978-0-692-86155-4

TO HELL WITH HEAVEN

"Only when the last tree has died
and the last river has been poisoned
and the last fish to be caught
will we realize that we cannot eat money."
- Cree Proverb

"Life's a joke! Die laughing!"
- Young Mane

1.

"This place is a real Hellhole," said some rat-faced man.

I agreed. Well, purgatory would have been a more accurate descriptor, but I had no intention of voicing my view. I was no fool.

The rat-faced man has been at it all day. Desperately blurting opinions in hopes to lure someone into a conversation. None of us wanted to acknowledge him. To acknowledge him - was to acknowledge we were here. Instead we retreated in our own shame.

"Hey! Scoot up!"

I felt a shove in the small of my back, propelling me to fill the vacant space in the queue. I must have been daydreaming. I certainly felt rudely awakened.

I had been facing forward so long I forgot who was behind me. I wished to spin and face the goon but a familiar, anxiety-powered-force-field paralyzed my body. I was frozen.

Hopefully my nerves would thaw by the time I have to plod forward again. I'd hate to be shoved the whole rest of the way.

"They know we are hungry! Shouldn't they have food for us? All I need is a little snack." The rat-faced man was back at it.

They should have food for us. I have been in line for seven hours. That's almost a shift at a fulltime job. Surely, cattle get kibble in the logjam before slaughter. Why not us? I was almost tempted enough to vocalize my support of rat-face's idea - tempted but that was it.

Luckily others agreed for me.

"He's right!"

"Yeah, I mean, they give free meals to prisoners!"

"Shut up! You're going to get us all in trouble!"

For the first time in seven hours – the line was alive. Security robots descended upon us from all angles.

"Quiet down!" threatened a pig-headed cop. He was the only human security guard and sadly he seemed the least sympathetic member of the force.

He shook a canister in his hand. The menacing gesture silenced everyone.

The security robots melded back into the walls.

"Aww, I bet that wasn't even mace. It didn't even make that sound," said the rat-faced man

"Shhh." reminded everyone.

"What sound?" demanded a confused woman.

"The shaking sound."

"Shhh!"

The rat-faced man had confused mace with spray paint. The confused woman didn't understand what sound he was referring to because he was wrong to begin with. He meant the clacking sound the metallic pea makes inside a spray paint can when the user shakes it up. I could easily speak up and correct all of this. It would be the fastest way to shut them up.

"You know, like this," the rat-faced man prepared invisible martini, "clacka-clacka-clacka."

"Shhh!"

"Whatever," the confused woman was no longer confused. She was now an indifferent woman.

"Shhh!"

"You know, like a maraca."

"Shhh!"

The indifferent woman no longer had anything to comment. Perhaps she caught on to the spray paint can confusion.

"This place is a real Hellhole!"

"That's enough out of you!" the pig-headed cop was back, assisting rat-face out of our single-file. "You're coming with me."

"Hey! Stop!"

It was no use. The cop had a firm grasp on rat-face's arms. He twisted him away with ease, allowing gravity and physiology to do the grunt work.

I felt bad for the man. All he wanted was something to eat.

The line continues to trickle. We are seen one-by-one. Slowly seeping into the warm air left by one another. I wonder what our queue looked like from the security camera's point-of-view. It must look the same all day. After all, you never notice the individual scales of a snake, do you? You simply see the whole, slowly slithering forward.

There are only a few people left ahead of me. My mouth is watering. I am so hungry that the anticipation for food stamps has now equated the anticipation of food itself.

Another shove. The drool slavered out of my mouth. I wanted to turn to complain but my nerves were locked up again.

A distant memory kicked its way back into my head. In the recollection: I am young, but old enough to know better. Old enough to know ghosts aren't real. I am lying in bed; I woke up because of a noise in my room. To fall back asleep, all I need to do is turn and face the direction the noise came from. I will see nothing there and my fears can return to their nasty lodgings within my brain. However, I can't turn. I can't move at all. Without the sanity that vision could provide - my fears run amok, painting an array of monsters, ghosts, and killers, licking their lips in the silence behind me. It was a nightmare, although I wasn't asleep. In fact, I stayed up all night, sweating and because I never got to snap out of it - I've been frozen in that nightmare my whole life.

My genetics designed me to be the perfect victim, keeping me frozen long enough for a predator to eat me alive.

My stomach growled. The thought of being eaten alive made me hungry again.

Up ahead, at one of the desks, a man crumples his paperwork. I can't hear what he says until the security guard drags him past me.

"My children haven't eaten in five days!" cried the crumpler.

"Shud up!"

Everyone kept their eyes on the backs of the person in front of them. I wasn't any different. I was too afraid to look at him, too afraid to see myself in him.

The man ahead of me marched forward to fill the vacancy left by the man with starving children. There was no longer any shoulders in front of me. I was the head of the snake.

The next open teller beckoned me over with a gesture that resembled one a witch would give a kid in a cartoon. "Come here my pretty," I imagined his finger saying.

I obeyed and followed the finger.

"Hello." I said.

He didn't hear me.

My teller was too busy exchanging banter with his cohort; she was stuffing her face with corn chips and nodding. I wanted my teller's attention but craved that fat lady's chips more.

"Excuse me," I tapped on the glass.

My teller didn't look at me. Instead, he continued his story, allowing his finger to do his talking again. This time the gesture was a simple extended finger, pointing skyward. "Hold on a fucking minute," I imagined his finger saying.

I obeyed the finger.

I counted to sixty, then seventy, then eighty, but the teller was still yapping. I didn't know how to play it. Was he hoping I'd make a demand? Show him that I truly need these food stamps. Was he hoping I'd beg? Show him that he was truly in control of my future.

I kept gawking, watching the fat lady eat.

Corn chips - I couldn't remember the last time I ate any. Corn chips aren't food; they are flavor. They are the least luxurious luxury humans have created. Yet here they were, dancing their way down this lady's gullet. Occasionally she sucks the residue off her stained fingers. Whatever flavor those chips are, this lady wasn't going to miss a single morsel of it.

It wasn't long before I was daydreaming her savory fingers tickling my mouth.

"Excuse me," I tapped on the glass again.

"Look Buddy! Wait your turn, alright?"

"It is my turn."

My teller turns back to his coworker.

"Awww, I'll tell you about it later." Now facing me. "So, let's see your paperwork."

I forked it over.

"No, no. This is all wrong. Mr. Ankeny, is it? You filled out the wrong form."

"What?" I begged. "I filled that form out last time, I remembered the form name: F-101. There must be a mistake."

"No mistake, Buddy! You gotta fill this form out." He slid a thickset of paperwork at me.

The form said H-202. I stared at the word 'housing' on the top.

"But, this form says 'housing'. I came to apply for food stamps."

"Hey, Buddy! Are you accusing me of not knowing how to do my job?"

"No, look, I am sorry." I pulled my pen out of my pocket and filled out the new form. "I'll take care of it, Sir!"

"You can't fill that out here! It isn't fair to the others in line."

"I'll only be a second, I promise."

My hands pirouetted ink into various particulars about myself.

The teller wagged his finger side-to-side in front of my face.

"No, no, no! End of the line!" barked the teller and his finger.

I floated past the end of the line and right out the front door without exerting much effort – all thanks to the pig-headed cop.

There wasn't any dust on my clothes but I felt the urge to brush them before I stood up. My watch informed me the food stamps office would only be open for another twenty-five minutes.

I'd have to try again tomorrow.

2.

The real Hell was the eastside of Los Angeles.

I wondered where rat-face scurried off? Surely, he'd agree that the food stamps office, as awful as it is, is a nicer place to be than the streets. At least the food stamps office had a sense of order, a sense of safety. At least they had air conditioning.

The setting sun boiled the piss in the streets, sending a hot vapor into everyone's nose. I never minded the smell. The brain will stop processing it after a while. It was the screams that got to me. The brain didn't have any tricks for keeping out screams, instead it seemed to log them and play them back when you least wanted to hear them again.

The fiery downtown air was always full of screams. Not only the yelps of the mentally deranged or the bawling of the recently disenfranchised. I mean the screams of starvation - the screams of death.

I crossed Broadway when a collapsed man on the corner began to howl. I didn't dare turn to face him. I didn't have the fortitude to look, the sound told more than I wanted to hear. The man screamed nothing and everything. His stomach was eating him alive, sucking him dry. There was nothing left for it to consume but his vocabulary, his syllables, his voice.

The dying and dead were scattered all over the streets – piled on top of one another. The buildings above them were vacant.

Every thing downtown was hollow.

By the time I reached my bus stop my head was throbbing. A daily reminder that I should have ate earlier. Something. Anything.

The bus also smelled like piss but a different kind. It was untainted by the sun and the heat. It was less syrupy than the caramelized urine of the streets. I imagined the various types of people that would piss on the bus. My aching brain lumbered variations of both desperate and brash squirters.

I stumbled into my flat; instinctively flipping the switch that controlled my lights even though I already knew my power was out for the last two months. I wondered how long you'd have to do something before it became instinct. I wondered how long you'd have to not do something before it stopped being an instinct.

I locked the door behind me and sat on my chair.

My stomach growled at me. I knew the sound was my intestines contracting, pushing nothing but saliva towards my anus. I hadn't taken a real bowl movement in a week.
A scream from outside crept through the crack of my window and bounced around in the darkness.

I broke into tears. How long till I am one of them?

Since my eyes had nothing to see, my aching head filled the darkness with a slideshow of repulsive things I saw out the window on my bus ride home - a highlight reel of despair. They were sights I tried to avoid, but apparently my subconscious went ahead and took them down for me anyway. I tried to close my eyes but it only made the images more vivid.

A lot of people still think they control their brain, which is exactly what their brain has fooled them into thinking. I know better. I know that the brain is in control and I'm just along for the ride. But, why must it torture me with pain and horror? What is its end goal? What does it want from me? Isn't it me? Aren't I it?

I looked towards my window. The horrific slideshow followed.

My apartment was on the fifth floor. I wondered if that was enough of a fall to kill me. I had thought about this a lot but never seemed satisfied enough to test the theory.

Maybe today was the lucky day?

I stood up and walked to the window, knocking my shins on seemingly everything I owned. I struggled with the curtains and when they were open, the slideshow ended. I had real things to look at now.

A sea of people wandered down in the streets. In a long enough timeline I'd be down there among them, sifting through trash to find something to eat. As hungry as I am, even now, I can't imagine eating garbage. Not Yet.

I wondered how much longer there would be people left to throw stuff away.

A neon pizza in the distance smiled at me.

I opened the window, filling my room with cold air and screams. I leaned out over the human sea. Something inside me begged me to jump. I would fall like a carved figurehead cutting through the waves. I considered it a while.

Did my brain really want to kill me? Or did I want to kill it?

I couldn't decide for myself, so I went back into my flat and grabbed the phone.

"This is Lifeline, my name is Jerry. What seems to be your..."

I hung up. I hated Jerry.

My second call rang for quite a while. It must be a busy night.

"Hello, this is Lifeline. My name is Kevin, I am here for you."

"Hello Kevin. Is there any chance you could transfer me to Alberta?"

"Excuse me?"

"Alberta, she is a counselor there..."

"Sir, this is a suicide hotline, you can't make personal calls to your friends here!"

"I know!" I hated Kevin too. "This isn't a personal call, well, I mean it is personal in the sense I'm a person, and the call is about me, but I am calling because I am thinking about killing myself. I want to talk to Alberta. I have talked to her before."

"I am sorry, Sir. But, that is not how this works. I assure you I have the same training as Alberta and I can help you through this tough time."

"No offense, Kevin. But, we've talked before and I don't like your approach."

"Excuse me?"

"I don't know what it is. I don't mean any offense. It's just that you seem too happy. And I mean, well, that is a good thing and all. It is good you are happy. But what do you know about any of this?"

"How dare you? Do you know…"

I hung up. I didn't call to be lectured.

It took about seven more calls before I finally reached her.

"Hello. This is Lifeline. My name is Alberta and I am here for you. Please, tell me what's wrong."

Her voice relaxed me instantly.

"Alberta, I am so glad it is you!"

"Trenton?"

"Yes, it's me. I don't know what to do…"

"Trenton, did you call and request me a little bit ago?" She interrupted me. She never interrupted me.

"Yes, I am sorry, I don't know what to do."

"It's okay Trenton. I am here now. But, please, don't call and request me. You are going to get me in trouble. You don't want me to get fired do you?"

"No! God no! I promise I won't request you again. I am sorry, I didn't mean to. I, I don't know." I gulped. I felt like a fool for wanting to say this, but I said it anyway: "I only trust you."

"It's okay, I believe you. I am here now."

I loved her. I loved the way she talked to me. The thoughts of suicide always went out the window, without the rest of me, whenever she said: I am here now. I wish she were really here. I knew it was foolish to love a woman I had never met, but she was the only woman who really knew me.

"Trenton, are you still there?"

"Yes, I am still here."

"Good. What happened today?"

"I finally got to see someone at the food stamps office, but he said I filled out the wrong form. I think he was punishing me for interrupting his conversation."

"I am sorry to hear that. Why do you think he was punishing you?"

"I don't know. I should have let him keep talking, but it was my turn! I tried all last week but they closed before I could speak to someone. I was so excited that I might get some food. He gave me a new form to fill out but I don't think it is right, I think he wanted to get rid of me. I waited in line for seven hours for nothing."

"I am sorry you were treated that way Trenton. But, tomorrow you should go in more prepared."

"How?"

"Bring a pen. If you are going to be waiting in line seven hours you might as well fill out every form they have. Don't be rude, but don't take 'no' for an answer. If they request you to fill out a new form, well you'll already have it ready."

"I don't know why I didn't think of that…"

"It's okay. Will you promise me that you'll try that tomorrow?"

I looked towards the open window. Its bad breath called to me.

"I… I don't know. I don't think I can spend another day like this."

"Don't talk like that Trenton. Think of tomorrow. Think of how good it will feel to get those food stamps. What is the first thing you'd want to eat?"

The thought filled my mouth full of slobber.

"Meat, steak, anything!"

"Be more specific. What is the first thing you are going to eat tomorrow?"

"Eggs, scrambled and on toast. Bacon, a whole pack. Orange juice and milk! Maybe even a donut."

"Good, that sounds good. Now how are you feeling?"

"Hungry," I admitted.

"I mean about killing yourself. You don't want to do that anymore do you?"

"I guess not."

"Trenton, I need a firm answer."

I looked back at the window.

"Trenton? Are you there?"

"Yes."

"Close the window Trenton."

"Okay."

She knew me so well. I got up and did as she commanded.

"Did you close it?"

"Yes."

"Good. I am sorry you are so hungry Trenton, but you need to use it as motivation. Think of how good you will feel tomorrow after you eat."

She was right. She was always right.

"You're right."

"Can you do me a favor, Trenton?"

"Yes, anything!"

"Go to bed, wake up early and go get your food."

"I will."

"Good. I want you to know you can always call me, you know, but don't request me."

"I know; I am sorry Alberta."

"It's okay Trenton. I am here for you."

"Thank you."

"Good night Trenton."

"Good night Alberta."

I plopped into bed and stared into the darkness. My brain filled the black with images. No longer of snuff films but of food. In a way, both of them were equally miserable.

3.

I woke up earlier than usual. My growling stomach
acted as an alarm clock. It sounded like there was an
animal inside me, which of course, I wished there
was – a thoroughly dead and cooked one at that.

I made it to the food stamps office before they
opened but there was already a line around the block.
A few minutes later there was a longer line behind
me. A hungry snake grows quickly.

While we waited for the doors to open I witnessed
dozens of people walk by and then scoff at the size of
the line, announcing they'd try again another day.
They weren't desperate enough yet.

The security robots filed us in through the double
doors. Folks grabbed the appropriate forms and got
into a queue. When it was my turn, I did as Alberta
instructed, I grabbed every form they had.

By the time I was finishing the last of the paperwork
I was near the head of the line. I tried to stay positive;
after all, I'd have food soon. But, I was still upset
from yesterday and all the days before. I was
offended that nearly every form I filled out was
identical save for a page or two, which largely was to
be completed by the food stamp office staff. I felt
insulted but compared to the feeling of famishment it
barely registered.

Finally, I got waved over by a teller; it was the fat
lady from yesterday.

When I approached her I saw she didn't have any
chips, I was somewhat relieved. I don't think I could
watch her eat again.

"Paperwork," she extended her hand.

I offered her the F-101 form.

"I'm sorry, Mr. Ankeny, but this is the wrong form."

The teller from yesterday looked over and smiled at her.

"My apologies ma'am, do you need the H-202 form?"

"Yes, unfortunately you'll have to get in the back of the line to fill it out."

"Actually, I already have it filled out," I said, putting it in front of her.

She looked over at her coworker for help. He made a gesture I didn't understand. Today, his fingers spoke a different language.

"I'm sorry, Sir, but you'll have to also fill out the JY-206 form as well," she held up a large stack, "they are located by the front door."

"One second, please."

I shuffled through the mass of paper in my arms. I knew I had that form somewhere.

"I'm sorry, Sir, but you'll have to fill the form out while you wait in line."

"Here it is."

I slid her the completed JY-206 form.

She held it up for her coworker to see. She whispered something to him.

"Ma'am, I don't mean to be rude, but I have filled out every form you have," I placed them on the desk so she could see them all, "I know how many people come through here and I am sure many of us are quite irritating, but I am desperate, I haven't eaten in days…"

"You filled them all out?" she interrupted.

"Yes ma'am."

She looked at her coworker again. This time he gave her a gesture that I understood. A shrug. "I don't know what to do," I imagined all ten of his fingers saying in unison.

"One moment please."

The fat lady got up and waddled out of her cubicle and out of sight. I waited in suspense. My hands started to tremble when I saw her return.

"Your caseworker will see you now, follow me, please."

Victory was mine! Her coworker looked baffled. I wanted give him a finger of my own but I wouldn't dare jeopardize my chances for food now. Instead I shuffled after the fat lady.

We reached a closed door at the end of a narrow corridor. She gave the door two sturdy wraps with her thick knuckles and turned away.

"Good luck," she offered.

"Come in!" a booming voice ripped through the metal door.

I obeyed the boom and stepped in.

The size of the office was a lot smaller than I expected. The door barely grazed past the desk that rested in the middle of the room. Behind the desk, sat a portly man who was nearly all hair. The only skin I could see on him was his nose and the bags under his eyes.

"So, you think you're a real wise guy, huh?"

"No sir," I was tempted to tell him how low I actually thought of myself.

The portly man extended a hand; the tops were also thick with fur. He was a beast.

"Sit."

I sat in the chair in the corner. It looked dusty. The man shuffled through my stack of papers.

"Ankeny is it?"

"Yes, Sir."

"My name's Raskolnikov."

I nodded.

"So, you filled out all the paperwork, huh?"

"Yes, Sir."

"Says here that you used to be a bus driver?"

"Yes, Sir. For twenty-five years."

"You know driving is a robot's job now, right?"

"Yes, Sir." I was very aware.

"Seems foolish to me you'd go for a robot job."

"I came from a long line of drivers, Sir. My grandfather was a driver, my father was a driver, and even my mother was a driver. To be honest I didn't like it much but I didn't want to disappoint anyone."

"Well, I bet they are disappointed now, aren't they?"

I hadn't thought of my family in years, but Raskolnikov was right. If I was anything – I was a disappointment.

"Yes, Sir."

"Have you tried another industry?"

"I tried to be a mechanic…"

"That's a robot job," Raskolnikov interjected.

"Unfortunately, it seems most jobs are robots jobs, Sir."

"There is plenty of work out there if you're attentive enough to find it."

"I am certainly trying my best, Sir."

"You should have thought ahead, Ankeny. Even the old fogeys knew robots were going to take their jobs, they knew it for years. Hell, when I was a little boy we used to have movies warning us about it. I don't see why the American tax payer should be responsible for your irresponsibility."

I didn't know what to say. I felt everything crumbling away and I was frozen, unable to pick up any of the pieces.

"Well, what do you have to say for yourself?"

"I don't know..."

"It is clear you don't know! You're in here begging for a handout instead of out there looking for work! Why should my taxes go to help a freeloader?"

"Sir! I paid taxes too, my whole life! I don't want your money; I want some of mine back. Actually I don't want money at all, I just want some food!"

"Don't come crying to me! You should have tried a little harder to find a job!"

"I'm not crying!" although I kind of was, "and what jobs? Everyone got replaced by robots, why do you think your damn office is so full of people?"

"Calm down, Ankeny!"

"But there are no more jobs! Teachers, the Army, the Police - all robots. Bankers, librarians, accountants, - all robots. Architects, construction workers, building inspectors – all robots. Cooks, dishwashers, servers – everything. Every profession, every job, every person is replaced by a fucking robot!"

I covered my mouth; I couldn't remember the last time I swore.

"That's it! Get out of my office, you bum!"

A bum. Well, I guess soon enough I would be.

"Wait until they take your job! Just you wait. I can only hope they are more caring to you than you were to me!"

"My job! Take my job? Nothing here is digital – I'd like to see them try!"

He seemed very confident. It made total sense now, it was as if the food stamp office staff spent their whole days plugging up the workplace with mountains of paper. They spent every hour making sure machines couldn't replace their bureaucracy. It was brilliant in a perverse way. It was all an illusion; there would never be food stamps, only crags of incorrect forms too daunting for a robot to confront.

It was a good plan but Raskolnikov overlooked something.

"The robots may not replace you. But, when everyone is dying on the street and there is no more tax money - they won't need to replace you with robots. They won't have a reason to keep you open!"

I saw the look on Raskolnikov's face. He no longer looked very confident. In fact, he looked terrified. He knew I was right.

In some sick and twisted way, I got pleasure from that look. But, it didn't last long. The pain of being dragged out of the office by my hair quickly ended that.

"If I ever see you back in here, it's your ass!" the pig-headed cop threw me down, tossing a clump of hair that used to be in my head back at me. I flinched even though it was a ball of hair. I don't know if it hit me or blew away in the wind.

By the time I opened up my eyes the cop was gone. No one outside in line looked in my direction. I didn't blame them. I doubt I would have looked either.

I limped away. I thought about going home but there was nothing there for me. There was nothing for me anywhere. It was over. Actually, it was over a long time ago, I was just aware of it now.

There was so much I never tried. So much I'd never do.

I looked up at the vacant buildings that towered above. Now there was a good height to jump from! The last thing I needed was to survive a suicide attempt. They'd cast my broken body and leave me in the streets to fend for myself. I'd be worse than dead.

Up the street, off 5th was the tallest building I could see. I imagined a time before robots, a time when the architect of that building was human. How proud he must have felt to see that building, soaring above everything else. If he was still alive, which was a big if; I wondered how he'd feel to know that his building became nothing more than a glorified diving board.

Despite the soreness of my right leg I made the trek towards that building. I thought of my parents and of Alberta. Would they know I died? Would anyone? I wondered what the robotic cleaning crew would think of my shattered corpse. Would they think I fell or would they know I jumped? Were they programmed to think? Programmed to know?

Suddenly, a giant neon sign caught my attention. Sparks flew from the base of the sign, cutting out the blinking letters that seconds ago read – MORNING STAR.

It was falling. Falling quickly – towards me.

I could have moved. I had enough time but I didn't.
Instead I watched it fall in slow motion. I was frozen,
like I had been my entire life.

I was frozen until the sign went through me; a girder
knocked me over and impaled my spine. It was only
then that I began to squirm. Somehow none of it hurt.
A shower of sparks and breaking neon tubes rained
upon me.

My blood gushed out of me. I watched it escape, it
was finally free of me.

I am dying and for the first time in my life – all I
wanted to do was live!

4.

"Where in the Hell am I?" asked an old man with a white beard, it was as fluffy as cotton candy.

I blinked a few times and realized I didn't know myself. Where in the Hell were we?

It was too bright; I rubbed at my eyes.

Ahead of me was a large queue. It was so long I couldn't see what we were waiting for.

"Please! Where am I?" the old man was at it again.

He was quickly shushed.

I studied his face and his clothes; it almost looked like he was dressed in pajamas. I began to imagine a scenario in which this old man slept walk to, well, wherever it is that we are.

"Hey! Scoot up!"

I was impelled to fill the vacant space before me.

I spun around to see my aggressor. He was missing an eye. His suit was covered in blood. For some reason he didn't scare me. In fact, I was surprised I had the balls to turn and face him.

"Did you shove me?" I asked him, staring into his good eye.

"Yeah, so? Keep the line moving."

"Don't you ever touch me again, you understand?"

"What are you going to do? Kill me?"

Everyone in line burst into laughter - everyone but the old man and me.

I turned back around; clearly the one-eyed man wasn't scared of me either. The old man in front of me continued to swivel his head around, hoping to locate a clue as to where he wound up. I put my arm on his shoulder.

"Hey, Pal. If it makes you feel any better, I don't know where we are either."

He spun to face me.

"That doesn't make me feel better at all! Where the Hell is my wife?"

I didn't know how to answer that, so I didn't.

"Please! Someone where the fuck are we?"

A few people in line gasped.

"You're dead you idiot!" a voice from the back of line called out.

"Dead?" the old man and I questioned in unison.

"Yes! Now be quiet."

Neither of us said a word.

I refused to believe it until I realized I had a gaping wound in my chest. I reached inside of myself. I felt nothing. My hand was soaked in blood.

I must be dead. There was little doubt about that.

The queue proceeded slowly, almost unbearably. I had no concept of time. I didn't know what I was waiting for. Were these the Pearly Gates? I didn't see any gates around. I didn't see much of anything besides dead people. The line behind me looked infinite.

Eventually, I made it up front. There were few enough people in front of me now that I could see that there were no gates, in fact, it was only a desk with a lone man sitting at it. At least the food stamps office had more than one teller...

The man ahead of me, the old man with the white beard, marched forward to hear his fate. There was no longer any shoulders in front of me.

When the old man was dismissed, the teller signaled me over.

"Are you Saint Peter?"

"Jesus Christ, Kid! You know how many people ask me that? The name's Yee!"

"I'm sorry. I didn't know. I mean I don't know, well, what is going on here? Am I dead?"

"As a door nail. Now, what's your name?"

"My name is Trenton Ankeny. Is this Heaven?"

"Trenton Ankeny! Holy shit! Give me a second, Kid."

The teller got up and went behind a white curtain. He was just out of earshot, I couldn't hear what he was saying but it didn't sound very nice. When he returned two laughing men accompanied him.

One of them pointed at me.

"This him?" he asked.

"Yeah, it's him, look at that fucking hole!"

"Shit."

"Excuse me?" I started up, "is this Heaven?"

The three men started to laugh.

"He asked me if he was dead," laughed Yeel.

"You cost me a lot of money, you little twat!" spit one of the men.

I was starting to doubt this was Heaven.

"Okay okay! Enough of the sore-fucking-losing, fork it up." Yeel stuck out his hand.

Both men deposited coins and then went back behind the curtain.

"Can you please tell me what is going on here?" I begged.

"Not my job, Kid. Your orientation will start in a couple of minutes. Head through there, take a seat, and wait until you're called."

I did as he said.

"And Kid!"

I spun around.

"Thanks!"

"For what?"

"For not offing yourself. I made a fucking killing off you!"

5.

Behind the curtain was a land littered in skyscrapers. Everything so far seemed unreal.

Was I really dead?

A sloppy sign with the words ORIENTATION WAITING AREA hung over an alcove. I wandered over and took a seat among a few dozen Chinese girls. I looked around for the old man with the white beard but he was gone. There were only Chinese girls.

We all waited in silence, which was good because I wasn't sure if, let alone what, I could talk to them about. Occasionally someone would enter and call a name and then a little Chinese girl would hop off her chair and follow them out of the alcove.

"Li Wei. Anyone of you Li Wei?"

No one moved. I looked up at the man calling for Li Wei. He looked like he was dressed as a court jester; his clothing was definitely medieval, as was his facial hair.

"Fuck! Not again. Maybe it is Wei Li? Is there a Wei Li here?" he sighed.

Everyone was staring at the court jester but no one moved.

"Which one of you little bitches is Li Wei?"

Still no response.

"Alright, fuck it. Do any of you assholes speak any English?"

I raised my hand. His eyes shot across the room to me.

"You! With the cunt for a stomach, you speak English or are you just raising your fucking hand?"

"Umm, I speak English."

"Thank fucking God. Get up, follow me."

I did as he asked and followed him out the alcove.

"What about Li Wei?" I asked.

"Huh?"

"Weren't you supposed to help Li Wei?"

"Snooze - you lose, get it? Besides she is probably too young to know her name yet. She can fucking wait, it's not like she knows any better."

"That's horrible!"

"Well, I didn't fucking kill her, did I?"

"I don't know."

"Well, I didn't asshole, otherwise I wouldn't be here would I?"

"I don't know."

"Yeah, clearly. You got a lot to learn here, so I suggest you shut the fuck up, stop asking questions, and let me talk."

"Okay."

"Anyway, welcome!" he smiled. "My name is Loki and I'll be your guide."

"Why are you swearing so much?"

"What did I fucking tell you about all the questions? Swearing? Who gives a fuck?"

"I, well, I always thought you weren't supposed to swear."

"Fuck isn't swearing. It is emphasis. I am being emphatic, asshole."

"But, I was told my whole life that swearing is bad."

"Ugh! I'm sure you gotta lot of things wrong that's why I have to give assholes like you a fucking orientation. Swearing should be the least of your worries, okay? No one cares about swearing, the whole idea was that you weren't supposed to say anything mean to anyone, you weren't supposed to use words to raise yourself above someone, get it?"

"I guess."

"For instance, calling someone fat – not okay. Saying fuck – doesn't matter."

"Some guy just called me a cunt. And you keep calling me asshole."

"Well, we're already in. It doesn't matter anymore. Now, can I get on with it?"

"Sure."

"Thank Fuck! Now, what's your name?"

"Trenton Ankeny."

"Holy shit! Thee Trenton Ankeny? I can't believe I didn't recognize you! You made me a rich man today!"

"Why does everyone keep saying that?"

"You were Channel 5 material and it just so happens you were the subject of a little bet up here. You see, not many American whites make it up here these days, on account of you all being shitty people and well, even less men make it up here, on account of the penis and all that."

"So?"

"Well, you were a shoo-in, you know, since you never really did anything with your life."

"Thanks."

"Anyway, you were going to off yourself, we all knew it, we saw it on the TV. Once, people heard you were going to kill yourself and well, people started making bets. Luckily for me, you died before you could do it!"

"Yeah, lucky for you."

"Aww, don't be so sore. You're better off up here. Believe me."

"It doesn't seem all that nice."

"Oh don't get me wrong. It is a real shit hole up here! But, it is the best place you're going to get."

"Fine."

"Look, Trenton, we got off on the wrong foot. You and me are going to be real pals up here, get it?

"Am I going to have to have this hole in me, like, forever?"

"Fuck no! Once were done with orientation you can heal up in your room. Anyway, can I get on with it?"

"Okay."

"Fuckin' about time. Anyway, where was I? Did I tell you about God yet?"

"No."

"There is one. Well, there are a few. But, there is one in charge of this shithole. He doesn't really come by that often, once every few thousand years but he seems like an alright guy."

"So which religion was right?"

"None of them," laughed Loki. "Hell, all the ones I grew up with don't even exist anymore."

"But, then why doesn't God go back to Earth and set things straight?"

"Oh, God doesn't give a shit about Earth. Gods are making better and better things every day. They got bored of planets and creatures a long time ago."

"Then what is Heaven?"

"This is an outcome. Think of Earth as a game. There are some rules and depending on how you play there are certain results. This is just one of the results."

"What are the other ones?"

"I don't really know but there are rumors. But, from what I hear all of them are a lot nicer than Earth."

"So if I am here because I never did anything with my life, then how are you here?"

"I was lucky enough to have my head smashed in before I could do anything truly deviant. I spent my youth taking care of my family, working in the fields during the day and working in the kitchen at night. One day some men came to my village and raped the whole lot of us. Dead and all," Loki sighed, "seems like yesterday."

"I'm sorry."

"Don't be. Dying is the best thing that can happen to you! It's a one-way ticket off Earth. Don't get me wrong, Trenton. Your lifetime didn't exactly fall on the best of times but you had a fucking cakewalk compared to most of us. You never even had to kill your own food. Your whole fucking life you never killed anything, do you know how pathetic that is?"

"Hey!"

"I'm serious. Think about it. You spent your final days crying, begging for food, when all you had to do was go out and get some. In my day, we didn't have restaurants and we didn't have stores. If you wanted food you caught it, killed it, gutted it, skinned it, and cooked it your damn self."

"Well, there weren't exactly forests where I came from."

"Oh," Loki wiped away imaginary tears, "wayh-wayh, poor baby. Go back and tell that room of little chinks how bad you had it. I'm sure they'll sympathize."

I had enough of this "tour guide" and this horrible place. I swung a wild punch at Loki.

"Take it easy!"

Loki caught my punch and twisted my arm behind my back and shoved my fist through my open wound. He pulled on that arm with one hand and pushed on my neck with the other. He had me trapped within myself. I was a one-armed pretzel.

"Stop!"

Loki tossed me to the ground.

"Fuck you, Trenton. I'd say go to your room and cool it but I don't even know where you're staying." He flung a scrap of paper at me. "Here, take Li Wei's room."

With that he stormed off.

"Hey!"

I was alone and I didn't know where to go. I didn't know anything anymore.

6.

Heaven sucked.

I wandered for hours, at least I think hours, it doesn't seem like time exists here.

So far, the only positive thing I have noticed is that I no longer feel the scrapping pains of hunger. Granted I still have a giant gaping wound and therefore no stomach. But, for now, I am not hungry and that is nice.

The streets were nothing but infinite columns of housing, stretching upwards seemingly forever. There was no fog or clouds to obscure their reach. It didn't hurt my neck to gawk up at them but for some reason I thought it should and so I stopped.

No matter where I looked, it all looked the same. It was drab, boring.

I stopped walking. I didn't seem to be getting anywhere. I sat down, cross-legged. I figured I should be tired, at least from all that walking, but I wasn't. It was probably because I was dead.

I closed my eyes for a long time.

7.

"Get up you fucking bum!"

I snapped to. A tall black man stood over me. His face looked like it was constructed from a series of eggplants of various sizes. He gave me a few shakes, as if to wake me, but I was already awake. I never slept.

"Stop!" I yelped.

"Wake up!"

"I am awake!"

"What were you doing sleeping there?"

"I wasn't asleep, I was thinking."

"Thinking?" he huffed at me. "Dreaming is more like it!"

It felt like a dream but I know it wasn't – because I was in control. Maybe I was meditating? I didn't know what that was supposed to feel like.

"What do you care anyhow?"

"What do I care?" the eggplant-man stamped his foot down for each of his sentences, punctuating them with his boot. "What do I care? I'll tell you what I care: I care about you, laying on the fucking ground outside my house. If this place is allegedly going to fill up then the last thing we need is people laying in the streets. Besides! Look at your fucking gaping wound. You look fucking disgusting Buddy! I suggest you go home and clean-up."

"I don't know where I am," I whined.

"What? Where is your sponsor?"

"He threw me down and left me."

"You must be a real asshole."

The tall black man walked away.

"Wait!"

He stopped and turned back.

I fished out the paper Loki tossed.

"Where can I find this room?"

I thrust the paper above me like it was a flare.

It worked. The eggplant-man returned. We both looked at the paper.

"5,036,798,724," it said.

"That's a big number," I said.

"A lot of people have died," he said.

8.

I couldn't believe it. Somehow my studio in Heaven was worse than my studio on Earth.

It was a five-square-foot room, furnished only with a white chair and a TV. I turned on the set and watched for a few moments. The story seemed dull but the camera work was incredible. It sucked me in.

The character spoke and I realized I didn't understand his language. I kept watching anyway. He seemed to be getting ready for a big speech.

I tried another channel.

This time I instantly recognized the man on screen. It was Sherman Caruthers – the father of modern robotics. He was the biggest philanthropist in the world, most likely from guilt.

The camera panned around his head like the track was on a halo. It stopped once it was directly behind him. Mr. Caruthers was framed perfectly for when the door opened and a man in a lab coat walked in.

"I won't waste any of your time, Sherman. The biopsy is still positive. Now I know how you feel about it, but I really think you ought to consider..."

"I'm not taking it, Eugene!" interrupted Sherman Caruthers.

The aging black doctor fell to his stool across from Mr. Caruthers. He looked defeated. This was clearly the continuation of a long-standing argument.

"You are still overreacting to the side-effects..."

"I'm not taking it!"

"Goddammit Sherman, for once in your life will you stop fighting everything!"

"Never!"

I turned off the TV. The black doctor's words hung in the air "stop fighting everything!"

I had never fought anything.

I was afraid of death my whole life and here I was anyway.

My doldrums were thankfully disturbed by the sound of people talking outside my door. Life may be over, but eternity was just beginning. Maybe I could make some friends?

The door swung open, busting both the room and my hope.

"Alright Li Wei, here it..." Loki paused, staring at me.

"Who is this?"

Li Wei was a stunning woman. For the first time since I arrived, Heaven seemed heavenly.

"You're an angel," I smiled.

"What did he say to me?"

"Nevermind, Li Wei, this here is Trenton, he is our, well, resident TV repairman! He was prepping your unit for you, isn't that right?"

"No!"

Loki scooped me out of the room and flung me into the hallway. I almost went over because the railing was loose. Heaven was rickety.

"Now, enjoy your place Li Wei, you get settled and I'll come by later to take you out to dinner," he said shutting the door.

"H…"

Loki knocked the wind out of me with his fist. This upset me but I was relieved I no longer had a giant lesion for a middle.

"Shut up, asshole! Don't blow my cover," he spit in a harsh whisper.

Loki pushed me down the walkway towards the stairs. When we were out of earshot of Li Wei's door, Loki started up again.

"I swear to God, if you ruined my chances with Li Wei I'll break your ass, you understand?"

"What? It isn't my fault! You were the one who got me lost, where else was I supposed to go?"

"Alright, shut up!" Loki patted me apologetically but it definitely lacked sincerity. "You don't know how long I've waited for some new talent around here."

"You can date up here?"

"Yeah, you can date," Loki huffed, "and it is fucking horrible! I've been up here for almost eight hundred years. You know how many pissed off ex-girlfriends that equals?"

"I have never had a girlfriend."

"I wouldn't admit that up here, Trenton. Women aren't exactly looking to play teacher for all eternity. They want a real man."

"Oh."

"It'll be alright. All the real men are in Hell. Pretend you know what you're doing and you'll be fine."

I followed Loki down the housing complex and into the streets of Heaven. They were as empty as before.

"Where is everyone?" I asked.

"Inside. Everyone is always inside. If you haven't figured it out already, there isn't much to do up here."

"Don't they go to work?"

"No one works here!"

"What about you? What about Yeel?"

"Oh, this is more like an assignment, soon as you learn the ropes you'll have to do it too. Think of it like jury duty."

"But, what about money? What do you guys bet with?"

"Money exists, but other than sex it doesn't buy much. There isn't enough going around for anyone to bother coming up with something to sell."

"Why isn't there enough?"

"Because bums like you don't have any. In fact, other than the Chinese and the Ancient Greeks, both of which I recommend steering clear of, no one was buried with any money."

"What do they do with their money? Are their rooms' the same as Li Wei's? That small I mean?"

"Small, sure, to a 21st Century American. But, yeah everyone has the same place. I assure you, most everyone else thinks they are a suitable size."

"But, where is everything? The kitchen? The bathroom?"

"You're dead, Trenton. You don't need to eat. No eating – no shitting."

"Oh."

Loki stopped and faced me.

"Look, Trenton. I know all of this is probably pretty disappointing, but I can't assure you enough how lucky you are to be here."

"You keep saying that, but I don't know. At least the people on Earth interacted with each other. At least they cared about each other."

Loki burst into laughter.

"Care? Care? Did they really care, Trenton? Did you forget that fast? How many people helped you when you were starving? How many people cared when you got thrown out of that food stamps line? The truth is – Nobody cared then so why should they care now."

"You're wrong, people do care. There are still good people out there."

"Well, if they know any better they'll hurry up and die before it doesn't matter anymore."

"What's that supposed to mean?"

"I already tried to tell you."

"Tell me what?"

"Eternity isn't infinity, Trenton. There is a capacity up here and it is almost full. You should be happy you made the cut."

"Capacity? What capacity?"

"There is room for six billion human souls and at the rate humans are destroying the world around them, well, we'll be hitting capacity sooner than you'd think."

"Then what happens?" I begged.

"Everyone left gets a detour – a one way ticket to Hell."

"But, what if they are good?"

"Doesn't matter, it is the rules of the game."

"What game?"

"Dammit Trenton! I have an easier time teaching Chinese girls who haven't even learned to speak any language at all let alone the Queen's English. I already told you what game – Earth!"

"Earth is a game?"

"For the fucking third time – yes! Earth and every other planet made by the Gods is just a game, an experiment. It is all a test to see what form of life, what conditions of life are the best. Unfortunately for you and me, Earth wasn't as thought out as some of the newer creations. Practice makes perfect and all that."

"So what is this? What is Heaven? What is Hell?"

"These are outcomes - simply a way of tallying the stats. It has only taken the Earth a few thousand years to fill this up. In a way that is good, we were designed better than a lot of other places. There are rumors that most of the games ended in days."

"That still doesn't make me feel any better."

"Yeah, but no one cares how you feel, Trenton." Loki patted me on the back. "In a way, our feelings are a gift and a curse. A gift in the sense, without feelings, we would quickly eat each other like everything else does. A curse in the sense, with feelings, we expect more than what really exists and reality hurts. Besides, you are dead now, you can't feel anything anymore"

"What if Hell is better?"

"It could be. The grass is always greener, they say. But, I'm not exactly dying to see what it is like to live with a bunch of rapists and murderers. Are you?"

"I guess not."

"It wouldn't matter anyway. You can't change outcomes. Once, you're in you're in. Well, I suppose you could go back to Earth and change outcomes that way. But, there is no direct flight – so to speak."

"I can go back to Earth?"

"You could, but would you want to? It didn't get any better overnight."

"What if I do?"

"Well, then you are even stupider than I thought you were."

"How do I go back?"

"Trenton, first off, you're dead. If you go back, people are going to be pretty confused to say the least. I have known plenty of people who returned to Earth and let's say – for every miracle there are at least a hundred disasters. Second off, what the fuck do you want to go back for? What if you stay too long? What if you miss the cut-off?"

"What if?" I barked "Don't you see? I spent my whole life wondering 'what if?' and where did it get me?"

"It got you to Heaven, you idiot!"

"Yeah, but maybe it wasn't worth it. Maybe you were right earlier – I never did anything with my life. Am I supposed to spend eternity wallowing about what I could have done?"

"Yes, that's exactly what you're supposed to do."

"Well, I don't want to goddamn it! I want to live!"

"You are living. You are living in Heaven."

"I want to live a real life!"

"Look, I am sorry for dogging you about it earlier. No one had a good life down there – that's how we all made it up here in the first place. Whatever you think you can achieve down there – you can achieve up here. There are plenty of souls up here to interact with. If this is all about sex, I have a girl I can introduce you to…"

"It isn't about sex. Well, maybe it is a little, but it's more than that. You wouldn't understand."

"Trenton, I do understand. I've been here for almost eight hundred years. I have had plenty of time to think about things. I have met plenty of people, all with their own doubts and desires. Out of the thousands I have known who returned to Earth, only a few came back happy they did it."

"I don't care. I don't care what anybody else does anymore."

"Look, if you want to go back, you have a very small window to return, I'm assuming you don't want to walk around as a skeleton and I doubt you'd handle digging yourself out of the ground. So I'll help you."

"You will?"

"Sure. It'll be easier to send you back than it will be to find where your real room is," laughed Loki. "I got a date tonight anyway, the sooner I am rid of you – the better."

I followed Loki in silence for a few miles. I couldn't get Earth out of my head. There was so much I never tried. So much I avoided. My bucket list grew with every step. I want, no, I need to have sex. I want to put my toes in the Ocean.

After a while we walked by the Orientation Area. It seemed full, though I didn't see any Chinese girls this time. Instead it was young boys wearing scraps and young girls wearing burqas.

"Hey," I tapped Loki on the shoulder. "Look," I pointed at the children, waiting for orientation. "Where are the Chinese girls?"

"Asleep in bed hopefully, but tomorrow morning there will be more. Death tends to come in waves. Right now orientation looks like a fresh batch of Muslims. Must have been the handiwork of a suicide bomber."

"That's a gross way of putting it."

"You seem more upset at me for saying it than the fact it happened. I didn't convince anyone there'd be seventy-two virgins waiting for them up here. It is sort of ironic, don't you think?"

"What's that?"

"Imagine thinking that by blowing yourself up in a public space you'll get to Heaven and be rewarded for your violence with seventy-two virgins. Sure, they are pumping Heaven full of virgins but the bombers sure as fuck aren't coming along for the ride to enjoy them."

"I don't think that is funny."

"Trenton, do me a favor? Consider it a homework assignment. When you are back on Earth, I want you to look around, make sure you take it all in. When you come back... If you come back - I want you to tell me: what is funny?"

We continued the rest of the way in silence until we finally reached a blue door near the entrance.

"Here she is."

"That's it? That's all?"

"It's a fucking door, what do you want?"

"So, what happens on the other side?"

"I don't know for certain, but you'll hop back into your body, wherever it is. If you're lucky your body won't have a brain anymore."

"Lucky how?"

"You wouldn't want your nerves working. The last we saw of your body, it wasn't exactly in very good condition."

"Will I be able to function without my brain?"

"You are functioning now aren't you? Trust me, you're better off without it. The soul and the brain weren't designed to work together."

"I guess this is goodbye," I offered my hand.

"Hold your horses," Loki slapped my handshake offer away. "You don't even know the rules! How do you expect to get back here?"

"I didn't exactly know them the first time and I did alright."

"Don't be so cocky, Trenton, especially now that you are looking to sow your wild oats. There are things you need to know if you expect on coming back."

"So, what can't I do?"

"You don't get it. Sure, there are things you cannot do. But, it is more than that. To get in, to be considered good, you have to do good. Treat everything alive with respect. Help people. But, for the sake of brevity, here are the five major rules: Rule Number One: help your fellow man. Rule Number Two: don't turn your back on evil – conquer it. Rule Number Three: don't hurt anyone – whether with words, actions, or shitty behavior. Rule Number Four: don't kill anyone - that should be obvious enough. Lastly, Rule Number Five: don't give up – don't kill yourself. You got it?"

"I think so."

"Well, don't say that I didn't warn you. Ready?"

"As I'll ever be."

"Well, Trenton. I hope to see you back here someday."

"I'll be back."

"So long, Trenton and don't forget: I want you to find out - what *is* funny?"

"I'll let you know."

"I hope you will."

We shook hands and I entered the doorway.

Loki's laughter chased me into the darkness.

9.

I felt nothing. I saw nothing. Darkness. Silence.

Until I yelled: "Fuck."

I heard 'fuck' exit my mouth and I heard it reverberate around me. Fuck fuck fuck.

My echo startled me, causing me to fidget and bump into a wall I couldn't see. The idea of being confined sent my body into an instinctive flailing, trying to orient myself. However, my movements were halted at the joints. I was enclosed in something.

Was I buried alive?

"Help me!" I screamed.

I heard murmuring in the darkness. People were talking. Could they hear me?

I continued to pound my surroundings with my knees and elbows. The sound of banging metal was deafening.

A crack of light illuminated my feet. The metal echoes escaped out the crack and were replaced by blinding radiance. I squinted as the ground beneath me shifted, thrusting me into the light. I couldn't see where I was, but I could hear that I was being watched.

I raised my arm to greet my observers.

"Hello," I said.

"Holy fuck!"

"Zombie! Run!"

I heard a crowd exit the room very fast. I tried to open my eyes to see what was going on but the light was too much. It didn't hurt but I knew it should. I lay there and waited for my eyes to adjust.

"Is anyone there?"

The answer was no.

When my pupils were the correct size, I saw the room was empty. I was lying on some sort of drawer, naked. The gigantic crater in my stomach smiled at me.

I was in the morgue.

I hopped off the metal drawer and searched the room. A dead body lay naked on a gurney; the body was split in half from autopsy. I put my palm over the head of the dead man.

"I hope you made it."

I looked at the wall – the meat locker. It was rows and rows of drawers. I wondered how many were full of bodies. I wondered how many bodies made it to Heaven.

The room gave me the creeps. Though I was realistically the creepiest thing in it.

I followed the neon exit sign into a hallway. One wall was covered in lockers. I opened them until I found some suitable clothes inside. I wasn't too picky. I only needed something big enough to cover up my huge lesion.

After I was dressed I walked over to the mirror. It
was instinct – I wanted to see how I looked.

Boy, do I regret it.

My eyes were deep in my head. Dark black bags
surrounded them. I looked more raccoon than human.
My head was a series of cuts and staples. My skin
was so pale it was nearly transparent; I could see the
network of flat veins mapped along my body, useless
now without blood. I basically look rotten – and I
suppose, I am.

I stared at myself. It was me; but it wasn't.

The hollow stranger in the mirror stared back.
Neither of us moved for a while. Until we both did.
Our fists met in an explosion of glass.

Now there was only one of us.

Me.

I left.

10.

I couldn't smell anything.

The sun was out. I could see the heat refracting off the cement, fuzzing out the horizon. The streets of Los Angeles never looked so beautiful. There was vibrancy everywhere.

Cars streamed by me, a speeding parade of color. I had never considered cars much before, but there is so much variation between each of them.

Everybody loves to prove how different they are.

Occasionally, a car drives past with its windows rolled down. I catch a second or two of a song. Then moments later, someone tuned to the same radio station brings me the next few seconds of the song.

Music! Noise! It was all so beautiful. Everything was fighting for attention. Some sounds drowned out others, some sounds never relented, but they were all here – together. These layers of noise were once in a lifetime. They'd never be repeated in the same combinations, even if you tried.

I let my eyes and ears inhale life.

"Hey, are you okay?"

I turned to see a young woman facing me.

"Who me?" I asked.

"Yeah, no offense, but you don't look so good."

"Is that so?" I laughed. "Because I feel great!"

I tried to swoop the young woman in for a kiss like I was a hunk from a Brooklyn Kelly movie.

"Eww!" she batted at my head furiously and then ran away.

Oh well. I walked the opposite direction and head to the corner to see where I was - 5th and Figueroa. Not far from home – not too shabby.

I head up 5th and took it all in. I had spent years wandering these streets yet it was almost as if everything was new. The textures, the colors, everything...

The streets were still lined with the poor and the destitute but I was no longer overwhelmed by their misery. In fact, for the first time in my life, I saw their true beauty.

I saw a homeless mother singing a song to her baby. I saw an elderly man sharing a meal with a young boy. I saw flowers growing out of the cracks in the cement. I saw paintings on the garbage cans. I saw a man in a wheelchair, playing harmonica. I saw children with nothing, playing with nothing but their imaginations. I saw hope.

The more life you lose - the more hope you gain. Hope keeps lingering around no matter how low you get. It must be a dirty trick from the Gods to keep us alive.

By the time I hit 5th and Grand the people have spilled into the streets. A few drivers, who are clearly lost, slowly ford their cars through the river of people. You can see the tension in the driver's faces.

One man, driving a blue car shaped like a helmet, looks so scared you can almost hear his eyebrows screaming. He is so afraid of the people around him, but as I look around, I might be the only one who notices him.

Everyone else is too busy to notice the man in the blue car. Everyone is busy thinking about themselves.

Including me.

Here I am! This is what I wanted wasn't it?

The screaming is more prevalent around here. Deep blood-curdling screams fill the air. I am not afraid; instead, I seek the faces that made these sounds. For too long I ignored them. Everyone ignores them.

I remembered Loki's words: "Rule Number One: help your fellow man."

I see a man in the crowd, clutching his chest. Hunger plays the man like a musical instrument, squeezing the last of his words out of his windpipe. I run to him and cuddle him in my arms.

"I want you to know that while I can't help you, I hear you, I acknowledge you."

He replied in nonsensical and fevered cries.

"We are both human. We are both alive. I am sorry you are in pain, if there was anything I could do to help you, I would, but I can't. I am so sorry."

Tears formed at the corner of his eyes. He hears me. I am reaching him.

"I know this sounds crazy, but embrace this pain. It is yours and yours alone. This is your life and this is a big part of it. Life isn't fair, they always say. It is true and you know it better than anybody. Isn't that beautiful?"

I was bringing myself to tears too.

The desperate man mumbled softly, his words were too soft; they were lost in the wind. He motioned me closer. I obliged.

"Shut up, you cunt!" he whimpered and then he died.

It took me a while to realize he was dead. It was confirmed after a few shakes. I left him where he lay. I pray he made it to Yeel and even more so, I pray he never meets Loki.

I realized I never asked about praying. Did it actually do anything?

"Help!"

I spun to the sound. It was a young girl. I picked her out of the crowd almost immediately. Her gesticulations were maniac. I ran to her.

"Help!" she screamed again.

"What's the matter?"

She seemed to be fighting an invisible force of some kind.

"What's wrong?"

She clearly didn't notice me. She was stuck somewhere else, walking in a dream. I watched her dance and fight nothing. She was so graceful. Strength found in the brain and strength found in the body are seldom related - almost comically so. Something inside that head of hers wasn't working properly. Sometimes it only takes one bad gear to ruin the whole machine. But, could it be fixed?

If I weren't so absorbed with the broken girl I would have noticed that the crowd forming, was forming around me.

What is crazy? What if that girl was perfectly normal? Her brain may have a 'creative' way of managing and experiencing time. She very well could possess the next evolution of the human brain, but she is unfortunately stuck in a timeline where her gifts can't be properly analyzed and studied. Instead, here she dances, clawing away battles with creeps who have long since crept away. She was a victim of time - twofold.

"Help!" she begged.

"What are you doing you fucking perv?"

Was that directed at me? I turned and saw the crowd.

It was directed at me.

"Leave the girl alone!"

"Yeah!" some agreed in unison.

"I was trying to help. You don't understand."

A big lug muscled up to me. From the way his body held firm I could tell he was only recently disenfranchised.

"Leave the woman alone, you pervert."

I took a big step back.

"You don't understand. I am trying to help. I know this sounds crazy but I came from Heaven. I came back to help you…"

"He's off his rocker!" belched a woman with bright orange hair.

"I am not crazy. Anyway, it doesn't matter. I'm glad you are here and are showing such willingness to help this woman. Something is wrong in her mind. We need to get her some help."

"Help!" confirmed the dancing lunatic.

The crowd began to disperse.

"Hey! Wait a minute! Come back!"

"Help!"

The crowd ignored us both. But, I wasn't going to give in – not anymore. I reached for the big lug.

He didn't like that.

"Lay off," he brushed me away.

"So you don't give a shit anymore? You were about to smash my head in for that girl a few seconds ago and now you won't have anything to do with her?"

He didn't answer. Well, not vocally. He answered physically by throwing me to the ground.

"We all need help!" sounded an old woman.

"Yeah, I got my own problems to deal with," said the big lug.

"Yeah and none of you are going to fix any of those problems on your own. We need to work together."

I got back to my feet.

"You don't have it so bad. Sure, you are living on the streets, but you are alive dammit! Things are getting worse everyday and they are never going to get any better unless you do something about it."

"Who you preaching to motherfucker?" a bull of a man charged at me.

I dodged him.

"You!" I yelled. "I am preaching to you. To everyone!"

"What the fuck do you know?"

"Yeah, you don't know my struggle."

The crowd was back and they were collapsing in on me.

"How can you tell me I don't have it so bad?"

They were right. They didn't have it so bad, but who was I to tell them? Who was I to compare their pain? It was theirs and only theirs. I wish I realized that before I was surrounded.

"Listen, You have to realize that this is your life, whether you like it or not." I pulled up my shirt and exposed my massive opening to the crowd. "You don't have it that bad, okay…"

The rest of my speech was interrupted by the sounds of dry retching. The sound rippled through the streets, causing others to gag. Out of the hundreds around me, only the big lug actually produced vomit.

Now he was as empty as the rest of us.

11.

To enter my apartment - I'd either have to kick the door in or go up to the tenth floor to see if the superintendent was here. I opted to kick it down.

It was all gone. Everything was gone - everything but the stains. I collapsed in the center of the room. I didn't care about my furniture, I didn't care about my clothes, but I cared about my stuff. Where is my photobook? Where is my Brooklyn Kelly poster? Where is the watch my Dad gave me for graduating high school?

"You there! What are you doing?"

I turned to see the superintendent was in my doorway. When we made eye contact he turned as pale as I am.

"Tre...Trenton?"

I stood up.

"Sarkis, where the fuck is all my stuff?"

I could see he was trembling.

"Trenton. They say you died."

"Well," I thrust my arms in the air, "do I look dead?"

"Yes. I mean, well, yes. I am sorry."

"Last time I checked dead people don't speak Sarkis. Now where is all my shit?"

"They took it."

"Who is this 'they' you keep mentioning?"

"The police. They came here and said you were dead. They took everything."

"Why? Why would the police have any need, any right, to take my stuff?"

"They said you were dead."

"Yeah, you fucking said that already!" I was beginning to sound like Loki.

"I'm sorry Trenton. What was I supposed to do? They are police, I do what they say, not the other way around."

"Los Angeles Police – protected and served."

"Yeah," Sarkis was tugging at his shirt collar, "so, since you were dead, I had to find another tenant."

"Sarkis!" I jumped. "I am not dead."

"Yeah, I am sorry about that, but they said you were. So I found another."

"Sarkis, what are you saying?"

"I'm saying you don't live here any longer."

"Why not?"

"Well," he looked down, defeated. "They said you were dead."

"Sarkis, for the last fucking time. I am not dead. Here I am. Here I am in my apartment."

"It's not your apartment anymore," he was looking down.

"Why the fuck not? Where is this mystery tenant? I have lived here for sixteen goddamn years, Sarkis. I am here right now. They are not. They are not here. Are you telling me, after acknowledging what poor physical health I am in currently, that you are kicking me out, to live in the streets for someone who isn't even here right now?"

"Yes."

That hung in the room a while.

"God-fucking-dammit, Sarkis!" I snapped my leg at him. His testicles smashed between my shin and his pelvis.

He crumpled to the floor.

"Fuck!" I stomped.

I broke Rule Number Three. I wondered how many times I could break it. I stomped again. Could Rule Number One cancel out Rule Number Three? What if I helped my fellow man?

"I'm sorry, Sarkis. Let me help you."

"Leave me alone!"

"Here let me help you up."

Sarkis desperately kicked me away, flailing like an upside cockroach.

"I'll go get you some ice."

"No, please leave."

I opened the freezer door – it was as barren as the rest of the place.

"They even took my fucking ice cube trays. Why the fuck, would the fucking police need my fucking ice cube trays?"

12.

I was out on my ass.

I feared becoming homeless my whole life. But, here I was. I was officially a resident of the streets.

Compared to dying, it really wasn't that big of a deal.

Luckily, I have an advantage over my fellow homeless: I don't feel hunger, I don't feel pain, and I don't feel tired - at least not yet. These are basically superpowers. I won't have to scavenge for trash to eat. I won't have to worry about fending for myself. I won't need shelter. I'll keep walking. I won't be homeless - I don't need a home. I am on permanent vacation.

Late at night the streets are different. A cold breeze replaces the heat and the screams. The air is nearly silent. Occasionally you can hear whispers sneaking out of tents or drunken laughs echoing in flaming trashcans.

I stood in the shadows and observed the men around the trashfire.

There had to be a way to help these people. But, without money, what could I really do?

I turned my head and looked west. I couldn't see past the towering buildings. The westside of town is where all the money is. I bet there was better garbage to eat over there.

"I wonder what it is like?" I questioned out loud.

Sure, I had driven through the westside plenty of times back when I was a driver, but other then a few gas stations, I don't think I ever put my feet down on westside soil. It was about high time to do so.

I lumbered up Hill to 3rd Street and made my way through the tunnel. A war had taken place here - a war between the city and the people. The dispute was about what the tunnel should look like. The city wanted blank walls and the people didn't. After a certain height, graffiti covered every tile. In fact, in some parts there was graffiti over graffiti.

"Hey, I was here, I was alive and standing right here." all the graffiti said. The long white rolls of paint said: "Shut up!"

Unfortunately for the city, their equipment only reached so high. Their message was drowned out – there were too many other voices. Voices willing to risk more, willing to climb higher to get their message out there.

The loudest voice in the tunnel was across the ceiling. It screamed in red: "Eat The Rich."

The further west I walked - the nicer it got. After a few miles there were no longer signs of homeless or the poor. There were lights in the barred windows. I could see people inside watching TV or eating dinner. It was a different city over here.

Did these people know what was going on a few miles to the east? Did they care?

I thought about it for miles. When I reached La Brea, I finally saw a group of people I could ask about it. There was a large crowd on the corner, smoking.

"Hello!" I waved. "My name is Trenton."

People averted their eyes. No one said anything.

"What are you guys doing?"

"None of your business," coughed a smoker.

I hated that phrase. Technically, I had no job – so he was right, but he couldn't have known that.

"What if I told you - it actually was my business to find out what you're doing?"

"Oh yeah?" a woman challenged. "Who do you work for?"

"I am on a mission from God."

The smokers laughed.

"So, what does God have to say?"

"I don't think he has much to say. I got the impression he said all he needed to say or least wanted to say."

"Then what are you doing?"

"Me? I guess I am trying to experience as much as I can. See everything I never got to see."

"What's on your list?" laughed one of the smokers.

"Well, to be honest, sex is on the top of my list."

The smokers erupted into laughter again. One of the smokers shoved the woman towards me. She didn't find that funny. Either did I.

"Are you a virgin?"

"Yes."

They kept laughing.

"Have you ever cummed?" A smoker blurted between laughs.

"I regularly jack off to romance novels, the ones with Brooklyn Kelly on the cover."

The laughter resumed.

"Do any of you have any advice on how I can do it? Sex, I mean."

"Look buddy, I think your only options are a hooker or getting someone really drunk. No offense."

"None taken. Getting drunk is also on my list. Maybe I can get two birds with one stone."

No one laughed.

"Are you serious right now?"

"Yes."

"What're you Amish?"

"Are you on Rumschpringe?"

"Rum what?"

"What's he want? Rum? Jesus Christ buddy. I'll buy you a round, come on."

The crew of smokers led me into the bar they were smoking in front of.

I had never been inside a bar before. It was somewhat disappointing. It was darker than I would have imagined.

"How can anyone see in here?"

It was also really loud - loud enough that no one heard my question. The air was a combination of music and yelling. The yelling only existed because the music volume was so high. The noise to person ratio was all out of whack. Didn't anyone else notice?

"So, what are you drinking?"

"I'm not sure. What do you think I should have?"

The man signaled the bartender. "I'll have two drinks," his fingers said.

After some elaborate pouring and mixing, the bartender set two glasses in front of us.

The smoker held his high, "Cheers!"

"Cheers," I replied.

The drink didn't register in my mouth. I saw ice bobbing in the booze but I didn't feel its temperature. I didn't taste the drink either, which I knew was for the best. Nobody drank this shit for the taste.

My attention drifted from the drink to the TV above the bar. It displayed the words – Caruthers Finds Cure.

Poor bastard, he was better off dying.

"Damn! Did you see that?" my drink buyer almost elbowed the woman's drink out of her hands. "He fucking pounded it!"

I saw her mouth move but the music replaced her voice.

"Hey man! Are you fucking with me?"

"What?"

"You drank that like a fucking alcoholic man, are you trying to scam me?"

"No, I am sorry if I did something wrong."

He slapped down on the counter, laughing. His fingers called for more drinks.

"Cheers!"

I tried to drink slower this time, I paced my drink buyer sip for sip but I guess I was still too fast.

"This guy is an animal!" he slapped me on the back. "Two more!"

This routine went on for a few more drinks. I could see the toll they were taking on the buyer. His eyelids came closer and closer to touching after each round. Hiccups and laughter replaced his dialog. His tongue hung out of his mouth. This is what "shitfaced" must look like.

Somehow all that booze didn't affect me. It was probably because I lacked the organs required. I looked down and saw that my lap was soaked in booze. It looked like I pissed myself. I excused myself and went to the bathroom.

"Hey!" the drink buyer woofed "He isn't even drunk! You think you can fucking scam me? Come back here!"

I pretended I didn't hear him and drifted into the sea of bar noise.

The bathroom was covered in funk. Most men's restrooms were but this one seemingly took pride in it. Pages from pornographic magazines were ripped out and stuck to the walls, hopefully via glue. On top of the nudity there were hundreds of multicolored scribbles and on top of the scribbles was a fine layer of piss. Men tend to ruin bathrooms, but drunk men, drunk men seemed determined to prevent anyone after them from using the facilities ever again. It must be related to territorial pissing.

I rung my shirt out over the sink and patted my pants with a paper towel but the wetness was still very apparent. I still looked like I pissed myself, which of course I probably couldn't do, since liquid wasn't going to make it to that part of my machinery.

I was struck with a horrible thought: what if my penis was essentially worthless?

I pulled down my pants and investigated my penis for the first time since dying. It looked the same – ugly. Maybe a little more pale than usual, definitely damper than usual, but I figure that was the booze. I plucked it out of its tangled nest and shook it. I couldn't feel anything.

"What the fuck?"

I turned over my shoulder to see my drink buyer was watching me. I put my penis away.

"Sorry, making sure it still works."

"You fucking scammed me!"

"How do you figure?"

"You had five Long Islands, asshole. You should be puking your guts out." He charged forward.

"Look here!" it was no use, he already had me in a headlock.

"You owe me $20 you fucking scammer."

I tried to explain how I had no guts to puke, but his arms were around my neck too tight. It didn't hurt so I let him get his anger out.

"Fuck you!" he tossed me to the ground.

I tried to get up but my hands were stuck to the ground. The angry drink buyer peeled me from the tile and tossed me into a stall door. It gave way and I found myself sitting on a toilet.

"Listen…"

But, he didn't. Instead he guided my head towards the toilet bowl. I tried to resist, pushing my arms against the seat but he kicked one hand out from under me and I went face first into the water. His boot pushed down my head. I tried to free myself but that only caused him to apply more pressure. I decided my best defense was to play dead, so I went limp. It worked, after a while his boot left my head and kicked my ribs, probably to see if I was still alive.

"Oh fuck!" the toilet water around my ears muffled his words but I could still hear them.

After a while I plucked my face out of the water and looked around. I was alone again. This time I was wetter, which was good and bad. Good because I no longer looked like I pissed myself. Bad because I was now actually covered in piss – and it wasn't mine.

I head back out to the bar.

"What did you fall in?" asked a guy playing pool.

"Yes," I said.

I noticed my drink buyer/attempted murderer was still at the bar. I thought that was rather bold of him. I went up behind him and tapped him on the shoulder.

"What the fuck do you want?"

I stared at him. I wanted to punch him in the face, no, I wanted to smash his glass over his head, no, I wanted to drown him in the toilet.

"Well?" he gave me a hard shove.

I noticed we had the attention of the bar.

"You." I continued staring. "Outside."

"You going to try to fuck me, virgin?"

"Outside." I repeated and then led the way.

Half the bar joined my drink buyer. They quickly formed a semicircle around us. They could smell a fight, well, they probably only smelled urine.

"What are you going to do you little virgin?"

"I'm not going to do a single thing. Now hit me in the face."

"What?" the drink buyer gasped.

"Hit me in the face you fucking pussy."

"Fight! Fight!" chanted the crowd.

The drink buyer didn't waste anytime. He threw his arm back as if he was going to pitch a baseball and then swung forward with all his might. The punch cracked me right across the chin and sent me reeling but of course I didn't feel anything, so I regained my stance and took a step forward.

"What are you a little bitch? I said hit me."

"Knock his fucking head off!" yelled his woman friend.

He cocked back and stepped into it but it still didn't knock me down. I took another step forward.

"I said hit me!"

He threw another, this time without the big wind up. It hardly moved me. I took another step forward. This time he took a step back.

"Is that all you got?"

It wasn't. He tackled me to the ground and began to pummel my face. His weight was too much for me so I lay there and took it. I stared into his glassy eyes. I could see his anger drain out of him with every punch.

"Fight! Fight!"

I had never been in a fight before. Technically I guess I still hadn't. I hadn't thrown a punch, but I don't think I need to. I saw how tired he was getting.

I laughed.

"Knock him out George!" begged the woman.

The people gathered around us continued to chant but the louder I laughed the quieter they got. Then, the only sound on the street was my laughter, which made me laugh more. I pushed the exhausted drink buyer off of me and got to my feet.

"Anybody else want a piece of me?"

The crowd remained silent. I glared at all of them. I didn't know any of them but I hated them all.

"You all wanted a fight didn't you?"

I shoved the drink buyer's woman friend. She fell hard to the concrete. No one moved to help her.

I slapped a cigarette out of a man's lips. He took a few steps back.

"A bunch of pussies. The whole lot of you."

No one said anything.

"Fuck you," the drink buyer piped up.

I swiveled around on my left foot and planted my right foot into his head. He lay down and didn't move. The crowd started to disperse.

"What's wrong? You all wanted a fight, didn't you?"

"He's crazy!" yelled a man who returned to the bar.

"This world is a mess because of people like you!" I yelled.

People were only willing to fight battles they could win. That was the problem with everything.

13.

The sun was starting to come up. I couldn't
remember the last time I saw the sunrise. I sat down,
cross-legged on the sidewalk and watched the show.

The black sky slowly turned purple. An orange oval
began to emerge on the horizon, widening and filling
the sky with light and color. The process resembled
an eye opening. When the eye was wide enough the
iris was exposed – the sun. Then the sky melted from
purple to pink to orange to tan to blue.

It was a new day, my second day back on Earth.

I thought about yesterday – Jesus how awful.

Jesus… I forgot to ask about Jesus!

Why did I come back? It sure wasn't to get into
fights. Well, it sort of was, but it was much more than
that. I came do something important. I just didn't
know what that was yet.

It had to be something good. Especially since I broke
Rule Number Three a few times yesterday.

The silence of morning was disrupted; the day had
officially begun. At first only a few cars drove past,
but now, the streets are jammed with cars. Droves of
people still lucky enough to have jobs honked their
way to work. As they idled in traffic I looked in their
windows. Most everyone looked tired. But, some
were not. In fact, they were too alert, hammering on
their steering wheels because of traffic or hatred of
their job but probably because a combination of the
two.

Men and women opened their businesses. On my left, an old man struggled to push the accordion style gate in front of his shop. Next door, a woman yanked on a chain and her garage style gate opened with ease. Both metal structures reminded me of mouths. Mouths open, hungry, ready to consume consumers.

I stood around and watched. This is what I wanted for so long? A job? Everyone here looks miserable.

I guess I never really wanted a job so much as the spoils that come from one. I didn't want a job - I wanted money. I didn't even want money! I just wanted the things you could buy with money. So many hoops to jump through.

People walk by, shielding their eyes from the sun. I imagine a confused military man standing here, returning their salutes.

Everyone who walked past me had a beautiful sheen, light beads of sweat hung on all of them like dewdrops. I realized I was sweaty. I wish I could feel warmth. Or maybe I don't.

From my current vantage point, I can see the beach, the edge of America. Something about it calls to me and I listen.

I take a few steps onto the beach and sink in. The sand keeps my shoe as I try to continue my journey, I don't fight it. I kick both of them off and carry them.

I continue to stare at my feet as I walk. I watch the granules of sand climb through my toes with each step until I reach the damp sand. It no longer squishes - I no longer sink. I bet this walk feels real nice, which is upsetting. A wave crashes ahead of me, sprinkling my shirt with dots of salt water. I keep walking until my feet are part of the ocean. The

waves hiss around me. Foam flows up to my knees,
soaking my stolen khakis.

I can't feel a thing.

14.

"Hey! Are you alright?"

I opened my eyes. An elderly black man stood over me. He was dressed in athletic apparel and somehow he looked familiar. He gave me a few shakes, as if to wake me, but I was already awake. I never slept.

"Stop!" I yelped.

"Are you okay, Sir?" he kneeled down to me.

"You can't sleep here, you'll burn. Look at how red your face already is."

"I can't look at my face."

"I suppose you can't."

"I know you from someplace."

"I doubt that very much, Sir. Anyway, I am glad to see you are okay, please go lay under the shade, you'll thank me later."

He turned to continue his jog.

"Wait, no! You're that famous doctor, aren't you?"

He turned back with a puzzled face.

"I am certainly not famous, Sir."

"You're Sherman Caruthers' doctor, right?"

"Excuse me?"

"Sherman Caruthers, you know, the robot guy."

"Yes, I know. How did you know about that? It isn't exactly public knowledge…"

I clearly had his attention; he came and sat in the sand across from me.

"I know this is probably going to sound crazy…"

"Go ahead."

"I think I just found the reason I am here."

15.

"Hello Mr. Page! Couldn't get away, huh?"

"Hey Ken, is Sherman in?"

"Mr. Caruthers should be in his office, everything okay?"

"For the first time, Ken. For the first time."

"Whatever you say, Mr. Page. Who is your friend?"

"This here is Trenton. Trenton Ankeny."

"Hi."

"I'll have to check you in, Sir. Can I see your ID?"

"I'm sorry I don't have one. I mean... I lost it."

"I can vouch for him, Ken. We are in a hurry."

"I can tell, well, just this once should be fine Mr. Page."

"Thank you Ken!"

"Yeah thanks Ken!"

The campus of Caruthers' Innovations was enormous. Large grass fields separated all of the buildings. Despite his age, Eugene Page strode ahead of me, I tried to keep up but my limbs couldn't move as fast and fluid as his.

We had obviously reached the main building on campus, I say obviously because there was a statue of Sherman Caruthers outside. Plus it was twice as tall

as every other building. Every room we walked by
was empty. A giant glass wall revealed an unattended
conference table that could easily fit a hundred
people. All of these rooms were so unnecessarily big.
They exaggerated the emptiness.

"A lot of homeless people could sure use rooms like
these."

"Not a lot of privacy in rooms with glass walls."

"Not a lot of privacy in the streets either."

The entrance to Sherman Caruthers office was
ridiculous. A series of moving gold gears and cogs
lined the walls. It seemed more than opulent –
because it was. This place was literally nicer than
Heaven.

"Do you have an appointment with Mr. Caruthers?"
an android stopped us from entering.

"SecureBot, it is I, Eugene Page."

"Response undetected. Do you have an appointment
with Mr. Caruthers?" I noticed the robot had a digital
smile.

"Eugene Page, confirm."

"Response undetected. Do you have an appointment
with Mr. Caruthers?"

"Goddammit! Sherman! Sherman!"

"Incident detected," the digital smile was washed
away and was replaced by a flashing red light.
"Incident detected."

"Sherman!"

Sherman Caruthers peaked out behind a giant wood door. The extravagant height of the door dwarfed the brilliant scientist.

"What's the matter? Eugene? What is going on out here?"

SecureBot tried to shield Mr. Caruthers from the misperceived confrontation but Sherman deactivated the robot via remote before it had a chance.

"I have someone you need to meet."

"Him? No offense, Pal but you smell like you woke up inside a bottle of whisky."

"No offense taken. It is a honor to meet you, Sir."

"This here is Trenton Ankeny, he has something important to tell you." Eugene looked back at me. "Go ahead."

"Why is that door so tall?"

"What?"

"Trenton, tell him what you told me."

"It seems stupid to have a door that tall. I mean nobody can be that tall. It seems like a waste of space. Why don't you have another floor on top of this one? You could have an extra floor and still have a pretty tall door, at least a more reasonable…"

"Who is this drunk asshole?" interrupted Caruthers.

"I'm not drunk."

"Jesus, Trenton! Show him already."

"Show me what?"

I lifted up my shirt and showed him.

"I tried to get drunk, but it didn't work because I don't have anything that booze can sit in," I poked what was left of my guts, "see."

"My God!"

"This man has cured death, Sherman. Can you imagine the implications?"

"That isn't exactly true," I said. "I lied earlier, I said it because I had to meet you Mr. Caruthers. I don't know exactly where to begin, but I have something really important to tell you."

"Come into my office, I think I need to sit down."

Various robots lined the walls, none of them were 'on' but they made me uncomfortable.

I hated robots.

"Trenton, what the Hell is going on?" asked Eugene.

"I know this is going to sound crazy, actually, I really should stop starting it off with that, I feel like even though it is suppose to make me sound more sane by acknowledging…"

"Trenton!"

"Sorry, anyway. Like I was saying," I pulled my shirt up to remind them. "I actually died. I went to Heaven and it was a real shithole, but worse, I found out it is going to fill up. Like there is a capacity." I stopped and watched for them to respond.

Did they believe me?

"Go on," encouraged Caruthers.

"There is a capacity to Heaven – six billion human souls. They figure at their current pace they will be full before the year ends."

"If any of this is true, what do you expect me to do about it?"

"I don't expect you to do anything. I don't think there is anything you could do anyway."

"Then why are you telling me this?"

"When I was in Heaven, I turned on a TV and you were on it. Both of you. I saw that you are dying…"

"Was dying. Our team has amended that situation for now."

"Exactly, I caught that on the news. But, I was hoping I could make you reconsider."

"Reconsider what? Living?

"Yes."

Eugene was shaking his head through all of this. I could sense how embarrassed he was.

"What? Do you want me to jump out the window?" laughed Caruthers.

"No! You can't kill yourself that is against the rules."

"Trenton, if Heaven is going to fill up, then why in the Hell did you leave?"

"To be honest, I came back to have fun. The whole reason I got into Heaven in the first place was because I avoided everything when I was alive. I died a virgin! But, the joke is on me, I can't feel anything anymore. I can't enjoy the things I came back for. But, what I told you on the beach was true. Well, the part about having a purpose anyway. I think I have a real reason to be here."

"Well what is it already?"

"I think I am here to convince you to die. I think I came back to help you get into Heaven."

Sherman Caruthers stood up from his desk.

"If Heaven won't have me, then fuck them. You clearly don't know anything about me, Trenton. I know my purpose; it is one I have realized time and time again. My purpose is to use my genius to help all of humanity."

"That's Rule Number One."

"You're goddamn right it is."

"You should be in Heaven. You deserve it."

"Nobody deserves anything, Trenton. That's why my work is so important. I would rather miss out on the Heaven you described, especially if it means I spent every waking moment I had making Earth a better place."

"You could make Heaven a better place."

"Maybe I could do the same with Hell."

"Listen, you have to believe me."

"Shut up, Trenton. I believe you fine, I just don't give a damn."

"Don't you think it is pretty pompous to call yourself genius?"

"Hey, Trenton." I noticed he was nodding towards something in his hand – a remote. "Go fuck yourself."

The wall of robots behind Sherman Caruthers came to life. All of their eyes were a dark red. All for one, who didn't seem to have any eyes at all.

Before the robots dragged me out, I got one last sentence in.

"Hey Eugene, I am sorry for deceiving you. I only wanted to help you both. It's not too late to take my advice, you know? Don't miss out because your asshole boss."

"Force level ten," commanded Caruthers.

I only had three seconds to wonder what it meant. At four seconds I found out. At six seconds I was nearly out of the building. Two bronze robots pulverized me into the ground and keelhauled me over tile and carpet. This kind of treatment would surely kill a man. Luckily for me I was already dead.

It didn't hurt but it wasn't comfortable and it was certainly less than ideal.

My chin and sternum plowed the large grass fields and the robots showed no signs of slowing. I was imitating a Bugs Bunny cartoon by the time they let go.

I heard the robots beeping their robot insults. The pulsating penetrated the ground; in fact, the dirt seemed to amplify the beeping. I already hated robots before. This sealed the deal. They probably were 'smiling' throughout the entire drag race.

I lay in my one-foot deep, self-dug grave. I laid there for a while, too long in fact. As soon as I realized Sherman Caruthers and his robot minions were probably watching me this whole time I sprung up and ran away. I gave them the show they wanted.

Sherman Caruthers tried to kill me, or did he know that it wouldn't kill me since I was already dead? A bold move either way – I honestly didn't think I could survive that.

I tried to vocalize my complaint but I was wearing my chin like a beard, draped about my neck. I stopped running to put it back in place.

"How the fuck am I going to die again?"

I noticed a lot of my skin was missing; luckily dirt concealed most of the damage. I was going to have a hard time convincing anyone to talk to me let alone convince them they should die.

There is only one way to convince someone dead - murder.

I rehearsed the rules:

Rule Number One: help your fellow man.
Rule Number Two: don't turn your back on evil – conquer it.
Rule Number Three: don't hurt anyone – whether with words, actions, or shitty behavior.
Rule Number Four: don't kill anyone - that should be obvious enough.

Rule Number Five: don't give up – don't kill yourself.

I was already banking on Rule Number One compensating for my poor effort on Rule Number Three. If One trumps Three, then wouldn't One trump Four?

"There's only one way to find out."

16.

I washed myself off in the ocean. Even though I couldn't feel it, I knew I was cleansed, by the rhythm of the waves. I walked to dry sand and sat down on the beach.

Somehow it was louder here than downtown. Louder but more peaceful. The screams of the ocean sound beautiful to human ears. It calls to us. It invites in, deeper and deeper.

A singing man and his acoustic guitar join the sounds of crashing waves. The song he sings sounds familiar somehow but I can't place it. His version is slow, sad.

The combination of sounds, the song and the waves, it stirred me, I collapsed. I couldn't feel but I could hear.

"...xxx xxx xxxxxxx."

I found out I could cry.

The singing faded away and it was only the guitar and the waves. Then it was only the waves. I sat back upright.

"Thank you," I said to the ocean.

This wasn't much but it was enough.

I replaced the tears in my eye with sand.

A couple of couples, meaning two dates on a date walked by me. The first set ignored me, refusing to look in my vicinity. The second set saw me, the woman snorted, she recoiled at the sight of me so violently that her nose tried to retreat too.

"Here you go, Chief."

The man in the second set tossed me some coins. The sand absorbed their sound. I looked down and pooled the coins into my hands - $2.45.

It was time to get to work.

17.

"Hello, this is Lifeline. My name is Kevin, I am here for you."

"Hello Kevin. It is good to hear your voice. Do you remember me?"

"Not yet friend, keep talking and I'll see if I can remember."

"I called about a few weeks ago, I was real depressed. I wanted to jump out of my window but you talked me out of it."

"I am glad to hear you are still with us."

"All thanks to you Kevin. I really appreciated your advice."

"How are you feeling now?"

"Well, to be honest Kevin, I don't feel much anymore. It is rather depressing."

"I'm sorry to hear that but you should look on the bright side."

"Yes, Kevin. The bright side, I remember you mentioning that the last time. Unfortunately, for me the bright side is getting a lot dimmer."

"How so?"

"Well, I literally can't feel anything. That wasn't a figure of speech. I can't feel. You'd be surprised how many sensations you are robbed of when you can't feel. Also, now I am homeless and I haven't eaten any food for over a week. It appears the food stamp office is a sham and has no intentions of providing me with anything. To make matters worse, I have a few severe injuries, debilitating ones to say the least. It seems to me, death is probably my only hope."

"Don't talk like that. Plenty of people have it worse than you."

"That is very true Kevin, I have seen them with my own eyes. The problem though is that I am stuck living among them – on the streets. I can't seem to escape them. Their problems are beginning to become mine as well. I am not sure how much more I can take."

"Think of the people all the way on the other side of the world. There are people out there who have never had a house and they are perfectly fine. There is always going to be someone worse off than you."

"Perfectly fine, yes that is most likely how they would describe themselves. Let me ask you a question Kevin. What do you say to the man who has it worst of all? The person at the very bottom. What encouraging words do you have for that man?"

"I am not talking to him, I am talking to you."

"I'd still like to hear what you would say."

"I am not going to pretend anything. This is serious."

"Very serious Kevin. Let me ask you this, do you think the lowest man on the planet knows he is the lowest?"

"I wouldn't know."

"Well, Kevin. He does know. He knows very well. Every single thing on this planet is a constant reminder of it."

I hung up. I hated Kevin.

It took six more quarters before I finally reached her.

"Hello. This is Lifeline. My name is Alberta and I am here for you. Please, tell me what's wrong."

"Hello Alberta, long time no talk."

"Trenton! Is that you?"

The concern in her voice floated out of the phone like music.

"It is."

"I was worried about you. I didn't know if the silence meant you were feeling better or you were dead. I am glad to hear you are still with us."

"Thanks."

"I shouldn't confess this but I read the obituaries first thing every morning. There was a man with a similar name as you and well, I was quite worried."

"Thanks."

"Did you get your food stamps?"

"No. They don't actually have any. They don't really exist."

"What do you mean?"

"It doesn't matter, but I recommend not directing any of your callers there. It'll surely push them over the edge."

"How have you been otherwise?"

"Well, I got kicked out of my apartment, so I am homeless now."

"Trenton! I am so sorry to hear that. Let me look up shelters around you, where are you calling from?"

"Oh it's okay Alberta. I don't mind it. Honestly."

"There is nothing to be ashamed of Trenton. These shelters exist for a reason."

"Yes, they do exist for a reason, although I bet we have very different ideas on what that reason is."

"I doubt that Trenton. I know the world is a cruel place; believe me I hear about it everyday. These shelters exist because this world is unfair but they also exist because people care and they want to do something about it. You need to continue forward. You need to get back on your feet. You don't want to be homeless for the rest of your life do you?"

"No, I suppose I don't."

"Good, so what are you going to do about it?"

"I have a few ideas…"

"Let me hear them. It is important to vocalize these things, it will help set them in motion."

"I don't want to jinx it, but I met someone pretty important and well, a job might be opening up for me."

It wasn't exactly a lie.

"That's great Trenton. I hope it works out."

"Thank you Alberta. Me too."

"I am sorry to hear you are still struggling but I'd rather hear that than about you giving up. Hopefully someday you'll look back at this period of your life and you'll be much stronger for it."

"Me too."

"I am happy to hear from you Trenton, really I am. And I don't want to sound rude, but if you aren't feeling suicidal I should go, the phones are lighting up, there are lots of people who need my help."

"I won't keep you, but I do have something important to ask you, the real reason I called."

"What is it?"

"This may sound sort of crazy, actually…"

"Trenton, don't be embarrassed, you can tell me anything."

I *could* tell her anything. I *have* told her everything. That is why I love her; she's the only one who will ever understand me. But, I couldn't tell her this…

"Let me think of a better way to ask this, um, I assure you it is for this job, it is sort of like a homework assignment.

"Go ahead."

"Imagine that you know Heaven is going to fill up and only a certain amount of people can get in. If you had the power to pick who got in, who would you choose?"

"I suppose I'd pick people who deserved it, people who helped others, people who did good while they were on Earth."

"Yes, exactly, but who specifically."

"I'd have to give this more thought, Trenton. I am sorry but I don't think I have the time."

"I know it doesn't seem like it, but this is really important, Alberta. A few names would be very helpful to me."

"I suppose I would have to pick my parents first."

"Parents, yes, I didn't even think of that to be honest. Who else?"

"Maybe Rhine Lafayette, the famous TV doctor, he helps a lot people."

"Perfect, who else?"

"I don't know Trenton, this is a lot to think about."

"I know but please just a few more."

"I guess, Henry Clayborne, the inventor. Maybe Umatilla Harney, the old actor. He was always a favorite of mine growing up. I'd be devastated if he didn't make it in."

"Interesting."

"I'm afraid that is all I can think of now, Trenton. I really should go. There aren't that many of us here to field these calls."

"No that's great, this is very helpful."

"Maybe pick up a copy of *Humans Magazine* they are bound to highlight a few deserving individuals."

"That's a great idea."

"Well, Trenton. I am very happy to hear you are alive, I mean that. I really am. I am sorry things keep getting worse for you, but eventually they will have to move in the other direction."

"I eagerly await bouncing back from rock bottom."

"You will, Trenton. I can hear it in your voice. Have a safe night and I wish you luck with that job."

With that she was gone. I stood with the phone in my hands for quite sometime. I tried to imagine a face as beautiful and caring as her voice, but I couldn't seem to conjure anything.

Despite the late hour, cars continued to buzz by me. Their headlights illuminated the streets. I noticed for every car heading east there were dozens heading west.

I walked for a long time. Long enough that the only cars left on the streets were cop cars. Everyone was most likely in bed by now, or whatever it was they used for a bed anyway. They had a higher degree of variation the more east you went.

Occasionally a policeman would shine his spotlight on me, but they'd speed by when I smiled at them. Each police officer flinched before they turned off their light and drove away. Whatever they were looking for – I wasn't it.

18.

I arrived to the eastside the same time the sun was rising.

"Good morning, son." We said to each other.

A newspaper stand on Beaudry was opening up. I watched the old man in charge struggle with the string binding his stacks of periodicals. His salt and pepper hair resembled the newspapers he hunched over.

"Need a hand?"

"No thanks, Sonny. The day I can't handle this is the day I croak."

I believed him.

While he tussled with the string I searched for a copy of *Humans Magazine*. It didn't take long; the man on the cover was staring right at me – Sherman Caruthers.

I stole the magazine off the shelf. The old man didn't seem to be paying attention so I took a pen as well. I left my remaining change on the counter as payment. It wasn't much but it was better than nothing.

When I hit 2nd Street I took a left and head for the tunnel. It'd spit me back out to where I belonged, with all the other failures. Even though I had no sense of feeling, somehow I was convinced I was more comfortable over here. At least I knew where things were.

I sat down in Grand Park and combed through *Humans Magazine*. The cover story taunted me in

bold letters: "Sherman Caruthers Fights Back." I
didn't bother reading it; I already knew what they
were going to say about him. He was everything I'd
never be.

The rest of the articles were brief in comparison but
they were still chock-full of flowery words.

I ripped a page out of the middle and began
formulating my list.

The first person I had to put down was Clinton
Taggart. I knew of him long before I read his little
blurb. He was already famous for being a
professional baseball player as well as leaving his
wealth and fame behind to serve his country in World
War III. He became a household name when it was
discovered he carried two of his injured comrades out
of a warzone, dragging them over twenty miles to
safety. He was the only man in World War III to
receive the Medal of Honor. According to this article
he runs a school for homeless children.

The next exposé that grabbed my attention was about
Linn Ochoco. A Mexican immigrant who started a
company that only hires immigrant labor. She
struggled for years but recently the company was
rated the number one company in America to work
for. The write-up ended with: "despite her vast
fortunes, Linn still commutes and travels via
subway."

In comparison to the first two, Pershing Haig isn't
exactly deserving, but the last sentence in his profile
mentioned he will leave his entire $20,000,000,000
fortune to charity.

Raymond Mitchell-Steele was a real estate magnet
that recently started allowing homeless families of

four to live in his properties for a year without charge. That seemed nice. He should die too.

The next article highlighted the life of Schiller Liebe. "Through his nationally syndicated talk show, Dr. Liebe has helped over a billion people," the article read. I wondered how they came to that conclusion. I was tempted to leave him off but Alberta had mentioned him.

I set the magazine down for a second and tried to remember the other names she mentioned last night. I added Henry "Duke" Clayborne and Umatilla Harney to the bottom of the list.

So far the list read:
Parents
Eugene Page
Clinton Taggart
Linn Ochoco
Pershing Haig
Raymond Mitchell-Steele
Schiller Liebe
Henry "Duke" Clayborne
Umatilla Harney

It was a good list - so far. It seemed a bit short but perhaps that was more practicable. I didn't know how I was going to encounter these people yet, let alone how to kill them.

Still, it seemed like I was missing someone important. I tapped the pen along the missing skin of my forearm until I remembered – then I added her name to the end of the list.

Alberta Wygant.

19.

"Who the fuck is calling this early?"

"Dad? It's me, Trenton."

"Trenton? Fuck you!"

He hung up.

I stared at the phone. I couldn't believe it.

"I'm terribly sorry, I must have dialed the wrong number. Can I please make one more call?"

The Librarian didn't look up. She was so lost in her book, her hand was acting as her secretary. It said "we're busy" - I dialed again.

"Trenton?"

"Mom? Is that you?"

"Oh Trenton! Oh my little baby!" I heard cracking in the background, judging from the sound, my mother must have hit my father with the telephone. My mother's free hand did little to mute the receiver. "You hung up on our son you asshole!"

"Mom?"

"Oh Honey! I am so happy to hear you voice. Tell me its really you."

"It's me Mom."

"Oh my little baby!" I heard her sobbing. "They said you were dead."

"Who did?"

"I think it was the cops, I'm not sure. Oh Honey. I was devastated. I thought you were dead. I am so sorry."

"Don't be sorry, Mom. I'm not dead."

"No, I mean how I acted in the past, how we acted." I heard my father disagree in the background. "I would do anything to have that time back."

"Mom, I love you."

"I love you too, Honey. When can we see you?"

"How about tonight?"

"Oh, I would love that."

My father's muffled disagreement grew louder as he overpowered the phone from my mother.

"Listen here, you fucking asshole. You had you're mother in tears over your little stunt. But, I ain't buying it!"

A pause.

"I'm sorry Honey he is just upset is all."

I doubted my mother's ability to wrestle the phone from my father. I am assuming he either dropped it or threw it back at her.

"It's okay. You guys have every right to be upset. I'm so sorry about all this Mom."

"No Honey, in a way, it is a good thing. It got us talking. When was the last time we talked?"

She always looks on the bright side.

"I don't know, Mom. I'm sorry."

"We can talk about it tonight. Do you still live off 5th?"

"Yeah..." I lied.

"Oh good! What time should we come by?"

I heard my father protest in the background but I couldn't make out what he was saying.

"How about nine? I, uh, I'll have to clean up a bit before you guys come over."

"Oh nonsense, we don't care. I want to see you!"

More protesting from my father, I could only make out the word 'fuck' which seemed to be used in-between all the other imperceptible words.

"I love you, Mom!"

"I love you too, Honey!"

When I hung up I realized the Librarian's hand was still talking to me. Fortunately the Librarian herself was still engrossed in her book. I gave an imaginary tip-of-the-hat to her hand and made my way to the exit.

The Central Library downtown was a gorgeous building. It was one of the few libraries left in Los Angeles that still actually held books. I had to exit through the gift shop to get back onto 5th. I paused and looked at some of the books. They were too clean – no one had read them yet.

There is something weird about a book that hasn't been opened. Something weird but I didn't know what exactly. I picked one up and thumbed through it. When I was done skimming, I put it down and picked up another copy and flicked through that one too.

I wondered how many books were here. How many of these books have never been read? How many have never been touched?

"Hey! You can't read those."

"What?" I looked up to see an angry employee.

"I said: you can't read those."

"The books?"

"Yeah, the books!"

"I don't get it. What else would you do with a book?"

"Well, for starters you could buy one. Then, once it is yours, you can do whatever you please with it."

"Why would I buy a book when there are thousands of free ones in here?"

"I don't know, Pal. Why would you? Here's a better question for you: Why would a man who wants free books and is offended at the thought for paying for them, be in the paying section in the first place?"

"Fuck, fine." I set the book back.

"I don't make the rules."

"No, I'd imagine you don't. But, you do enforce them. You might want to ask yourself: Which is worse?"

When I got outside I could see the sun was licking its fiery tongue across the faces of the down and out. People held up their day old newspapers or their sunburned hands to protect their faces but it was futile. The heat merely went around the object and drooled down its victim's foreheads. I stared and watched these people. I wondered why they didn't get up and move to the shade, or walk out of the sun and into the library.

A giant clock tower informed me I had eight hours until my parents came over for dinner. I needed a weapon.

"How in Hell am I going to kill my parents?"

A homeless man overheard me and frowned. I gave him a wave and walked away.

I kept thinking about books. They were a lot like the marginalized people lining the streets – the sidewalks were their shelves, they weren't going anywhere until someone needed something of them.

How many books were there? How many books could there be? How many of them have never been written?

After walking for a couple of miles, I arrived in Westlake. Despite the searing heat, the streets were packed full of people. My pace seriously diminished when I crossed Alvarado. Men and women, young and old, bumped by me. I couldn't feel their shoves and nudges, but I could tell it was happening from the frequency in which my view was altered.

I stopped on the corner but the flowing masses rotated me like I was a turnstile. I didn't mind, it allowed me to look at all the signs. The high-density of businesses in Westlake was overwhelming. Signs, like their businesses, were stacked on top of one another. The various pastel outlines, dividing each business, resembled mounds of ice cream scoops, towering above the streets. The ice cream look was strengthened by the fact that all the sloppy paint jobs appeared to be melting.

A cute sign reading: 'An Easy Pet' caught my eye. Their logo was meant to resemble a hand of poker, but instead of spades or clubs, the cards were marked with cat or dog paw prints. I walked up four flights of stairs and walked inside.

An Easy Pet was an absolute mess inside. The inventory was heavily picked through. There seemed to be more products on the floor than on the shelves. Luckily for the animals, their section was a little tidier.

The dogs were the first to be aware of my presence. They filled the air with a series of barks that pleaded: "Hey! Get me out of here!" I made the mistake of looking at them. All they wanted was to be out and loved. Their wet and sad eyes were tragic, but no more tragic than the watery eyes lining the blocks outside. It seemed everything alive was equally miserable.

The dogs were in and wanted out. The humans were out and wanted in. They all wanted love but not from where they got it, but from where they *could* get it.

I started doubting my previous views on hope. Hope wasn't beautiful - hope was a plague.

Everyone figures the grass is greener on the other side. But, there is no grass. There is no grass on either side.

"Can I help you?"

I noticed the shriveled woman was nearly camouflaged by her merchandise.

"Do you have any poison?"

"No poison."

"Do you have anything that could be poisonous?"

"No poison."

"Are you sure?"

"Yes, I'm sure. No poison!"

"Do you know where I might be able to find some?"

"Try poison store."

"I don't think that's a thing."

I looked over at the dogs again. They were still watching me; their wagging tails banged their cages like old timey criminals dragging their empty cups along the bars. They wanted my attention. The fools. Perhaps it was because they had dog brains but they didn't seem to realize they had everything they needed already. They had free food. There were enough dogs to keep one another busy.

They'd be a lot happier if they focused on each other, loved one another. Years of breeding has programmed these animals into thinking they needed humans, but they don't, they never did.

I walked towards their cages; it caused each dog to set into a whimper that collectively sounded like the whistle of air escaping a boiling kettle. A whistle that evolved over time to reach the high notes, where the human heartstrings reside. So pitch perfect - it worked on a man who may or may not have a heart anymore.

When I was closer, the whimpers morphed into growls. Saliva poured out of their mouths. The largest dog clawed at his cage aggressively.

I realized these dogs didn't want my love. They could smell the stench of my open wound. They wanted my guts.

I slowly backed out of the store.

From my vantage point I could see directly into MacArthur Park. Despite being surrounded by things like the 99-Cent Store and Yoshinoya Beef Bowl, it was gorgeous.

It was also one of the best places to get killed or robbed in Los Angeles but since I was dead and didn't have anything, I wasn't too worried about it.

I could only see the beauty. It was a green oasis - a lake in the middle of Hell.

There was a hardware store across the street. They were bound to have something to kill my parents with.

The concrete veldt before the hardware store was rife with men looking for work, hassling every passerby with what they could offer and how eager they were to do it. As each one of them obstructed my journey, I looked into their eyes. I could see their desperation.

Here were men who could make an entire house from scratch. But, none of them had one. They could build their own but where would they put it? Someone would eventually come along and say, "Hey, you can't live here, I own this dirt you're on."

Zealous, commission-hungry employees swarmed the aisles of the hardware store. They were more aggressive than their outdoor counterparts. It was probably due to the luxury of air conditioning.

"Ah Jeez, are you alright, Mister?"

"Who me?"

"Yeah…"

"I'm fine."

"You look like you were in an accident."

"Well, I think that is rather rude of you to say."

"I'm sorry, I was, I just wanted to know if you needed help."

"Well, I appreciate that. That is actually very nice of you."

"Thanks. Anyway, sorry."

"Hey!" I called out.

He turned over his shoulder; I had his attention.

"I hope you die soon! You deserve it!"

He frowned and walked away.

I was amazed at how many hammers there were. Rows and rows of them, a glut of objects to smash other objects with. The smaller the hammerhead got - the more specific it became. It seemed like this sledgehammer could do the work of all of these combined. I didn't get it.

Every tool looked dangerous. Effective but brutal. I wanted my parents dead - not destroyed. As much as I resent my father, there is no way, dead or alive that I could smash him to death. Or saw him to death.

"Can I help you, Sir?"

The acne on this kid's face made my skin look good enough for a Jergens ad.

"I am looking for poison."

"Excuse me, Sir?"

"I mean, I am looking to avoid any, I was hoping, you'd have a different section for organic chemicals."

"Oh, well, I don't know if we have chemicals, we have metal though."

"Yes, I see that. Do you carry any household cleaners?"

"Oh, those are on Aisle 6. Follow me."

"I can find it for myself."

I shuffled past the human zit and over to Aisle 6. I looked for anything with a skull on it. I settled for Oven Cleaner and Windshield Wiper Fluid.

Half way to the register I froze in place. I realized I didn't have any money. Luckily I had one Hell of a pocket.

It took a couple of laps around the store before I found an area untainted from the salesman infestation. I jammed the boxes up into my ribcage and then tucked my shirt back in.

As I exited, the RFID labels on the stolen products set off the alarm. Two security robots appeared out from the walls. Fortunately for me, they were only designed to scan pockets and shoes. A human employee would have patted me down.

They still claim robots are more effective than humans and I don't doubt that many of them are. But, the reality of the situation, I now realize, is that you don't pay a robot. You buy it. Robots have no incentives – just programming. You pay the one time and save for occasional repair - that's it.

The robots gave their form of an electronic shrug to the manager robot. Some of the human employees waited for a reaction. The note of silence hung in the store.

If the manager robot responded I wasn't around to see it.

I left.

I turned my back on the setting sun. I walked east. I walked home.

20.

By the time I was on the fifth floor I remembered I didn't actually live here anymore.

I had completely disregarded a plan for the new tenant. Hopefully they wouldn't be here.

They were.

"Hello? What is this about?"

"Hi there, my name is Trenton, there must be some sort of mistake. This is my place."

"What? No, you're dead!"

"Do I look dead?" I put my hand up to stop him. "Don't answer that. Look, can I come in?"

"No."

I pushed my way in.

"This is highly irregular," he protested.

I slammed the door. I looked him up and down. He looked like french fries wearing a t-shirt and jean-shorts.

"Highly irregular is fucking right! This was my place asshole."

I surveyed the room. His furniture was worse than mine. A zebra striped couch assaulted my eyes.

"They said you were dead."

"Fuck!"

I swiped at the new tenant's potatoface. My nails dug off a layer of starch and he screamed like Hell because of it.

"Do I fucking look dead?"

I kicked him across the room.

The door flung open and Sarkis barged into the room.

"What's…. Trenton? Goddammit, I told you to get out of here!"

I charged him.

"A guy nearly dies and they get upset when he comes home! Just because I almost died that means I have to die? I thought we were humans. Isn't that what makes us better than animals – we don't kill our weak, well, am I right?"

I realized I was yelling at a corpse. Blood was pooling at Sarkis' feet. The coat hook was hiding in the back of his head. He hung there, useless as a jacket in Los Angeles.

I turned to face the new tenant. He was busy gawking at his own blood. Dabbing his face wildly and then dancing his hands in front of his eyes. A bloody jazz show.

"Believe it friend, you're full of that stuff. Let me show you!"

I landed ontop of him. I drove my knee into his stomach and choked him. His face began changing colors. It looked like someone dipped his head in ketchup.

I put both dead men under the bed. The back of Sarkis's head left a trail on the hardwood floor. The skidmark was like connect-the-dots, literally connecting the dots from crime to evidence. I slid the Oven Cleaner out past my lungs and gave the floor a once over with it and a shirt I found.

The clock caught my eye for two reasons. One, I now had less than an hour until my parents arrived. Two, the clock itself was framed in a vibrant pink vagina. It looked like the wall was winking at me.

"Jesus Christ."

As soon as I pulled it down, I began to notice all of them – the vaginas - all of the vaginas. The room was covered in them. I plucked as many off of shelves as I did off of walls but there were still dozens.

"Jesus!"

This task was more daunting than hiding the dead bodies.

It took three trips and three armloads to throw all those vaginas under the bed. I searched both dead men, taking both their wallets and Sarkis's cellphone. I opened the window and squinted ahead towards the neon pizza place down the street and dialed their number.

"Yes, can I order some pizzas, throw in a salad, oh and a soup, a big soup."

The girl on the other end repeated my order.

"Perfect. What's that? Oh yeah, I'll be paying cash. Yeah. Yeah. Up the street. Number 312. Apartment 503. Okay thanks."

I counted both of the dead men's money but it only totaled $46, which was $5 short of the bill and even shorter on a tip. I looked around the room. The clock was gone but I knew I didn't have enough time to go look for more money.

The place looked too barren. It was like the room had a five o'clock shadow, in the sense that you could see that a beard was supposed to be there, but it wasn't and somehow that looks more ugly than if the beard would have been there in the first place.

Realistically this was more of an eight o'clock shadow.

I rummaged through the dead man's still packed belongings, opening box after box but there was slim pickings when it came to non-vaginal related items. I picked out a few things and placed them about. I hung a few paintings. One was definitely of a vagina but it looked enough like flowers that it made the cut.

There was a knock at the door.

It was the Pizza Girl. I answered.

"Good evening, Sir. Here is your order," she handed me the pile of food. "Two large cheese pizzas, one salad, and one extra large soup," she stood there smiling.

"Okay well, thanks."

"That will be $51.50 please," her smile grew an inch on both sides.

"Well, come in. Let me set these down. The money is in the bedroom. Maybe you could follow me in there, it sure would make things easier on me."

21.

I had been standing, staring out of the peephole for some time. A couple appeared and I just assumed they were the neighbors. It wasn't until they started knocking at my door that I recognized the man.

It was my brother. Instinctively I tried to hide.

"Did you see that?" He knocked again. "I saw you in the peephole, Trenton. Open up!"

I did as he commanded.

"Tyler!"

I pulled him in the room with a bear hug. He tried to push away but I had a good grip on him.

"Jesus, Trenton."

I set him free and his momentum sent him tumbling into the zebra couch. I grabbed his date's hand and shook it assertively.

"Hello, I'm Trenton."

"Hi, I'm Ramona." I saw her eye twitch but she kept her smile.

"For Christsake, Trenton, lay off." Tyler pried me away. "You look like shit."

"I was in an accident."

"Yeah, I heard. Dad told me it was a load of shit but Jesus, look at you."

"Stop it, Tyler. He looks fine."

"Well, wait till Dad sees you, he's going to shit his pants."

"Tyler!"

"It's okay, Ramona. My brother has always been an asshole, I am used to it by now."

"What'd you say?" he picked me up by the lapels.

"What're you going to do? Hit me? I invite you over for dinner and you're already going to hit me?"

He let me go.

"Have you been here for a minute yet?"

"Aww, shut it. I was kiddin'."

"I don't know how long you have been dating this asshole, Ramona, but I don't think he's going to get any better."

"That's my wife you're talking to," he was back at my lapels.

There was a knock at the door. Tyler put me down and I head for the door. Before I could answer, there was a loud pound, most likely a kick, partnered with an exclamation.

"C'mon already!"

I swung the door open and hugged my father, disarming him the same way I disarmed my brother.

"I'd like to think you're so impatient because you miss me."

He easily shoved me off of him, discarding me back into the apartment. Fifty years of loading and unloading semitrucks, day in and day out, provided my father a strength rarely found in a retired man.

"Shut up. Where is the food? I am starving."

I held my Mom with both hands, holding her the same way you would admire a treasure. Then I squeezed her with everything I had.

"I missed you Mom."

"Oh Honey."

I saw my eyes were leaking. So were my nose and mouth. I left a damp outline of my face on my mother's sweater.

I couldn't do this anymore…

"Will you get a load of this place, Pop?"

"It's a fucking sty," replied my father.

"Elliot!" reprimanded my mother.

"Well, it is. It looks like a crime scene in here."

"Take a look at the couch, Pop." Tyler pointed to the couch by kicking it, as if it somehow needed help to standout. "You go on a safari recently Trenton? Bag yourself a whatever-its-called."

"Zebra," I answered.

"Yeah I know. I was kiddin'. Jesus."

I hugged my Mom again.

"I missed you so much Mom."

"Oh Honey. It is so good to see you again."

"Ah come on. You said that already. Where is the food? I'm starving."

"I still have to pick it up," I lied.

I can't do this. I won't do this.

"He said he'd have food ready," my father turned to my brother, "he said he'd have food ready."

"No I didn't."

"What kind of guy doesn't own a TV? Hey, Pop! Look at the wall, where are all the frames? I see the nails but there aren't any frames. You hiding something from us, Trenton?"

"Tyler!"

My brother marched toward a cabinet and dug through it. I jogged over but it was too late. Tyler spun around wielding a dildo, thrusting and parrying it like it was a sword.

"Take a look at this!"

"Put it away!"

"What kind of a disgusting freak is my brother?"

"Look, it isn't mine."

"Yeah right!" Tyler threw the rubber dick down and brushed his hands on his thigh; he probably realized how dirty the thing was. "You're fucking disgusting.

That's the sickest shit I ever saw in my life. Who would come up with something like this?"

"Well, I hate to blow your mind but guess what? They mass-produce them, every shape and size you can think of. Any color the human eye can see." I picked up the dick and marched it to the window. "They sell them in stores - stores found in every city in America. Hell, there is a street a few blocks from here; pretty much the only kind of store there is over there."

I tossed the dildo out the window.

"I know what it is, dumbass. I was just kiddin'."

"For the sake of not losing my appetite I'm going to forget that even happened."

"So Dad, what are you driving these days?"

" '69 Camaro. Me and Ty fixed it up last year got her running real smooth."

"That's great. I'd love to see it later."

"Yeah," my father looked away.

"Well, thanks for being here Dad."

"Elliot…" my Mom nudged him.

"Yeah, I said yeah."

It was going to take a lot of work but maybe I could change things. Without anxiety I could easily dodge past my father's disappointment and my brother's jockeying. I had a chance to fix this. Fix me.

"You know, I almost didn't want to bring Ramona along. On account downtown being so dangerous and all."

"It's fine, Tyler. I am happy we can all be here," Ramona smiled her fake smile again.

"I appreciate you guys coming down here. It really has been a long time."

Too long. Well, for me. They had each other. I hardly recognized them. Age. Years and years added to their faces. Years without me.

"You don't look so hot, Son."

"Well, Dad. I had an accident, but I am doing okay. I am doing better now that you are all here." I meant it.

"You should come out to Marina Del Rey sometime Trenton. You gotta see the view we wake up to every morning. Maybe it will inspire you. Inspire you to get your act together and finally get out of this dump."

"Tyler!"

"Do you have anything I can snack on at least?"

"Yeah, I have a salad, I'll be right back."

"Jesus! What're you making me wait for? I'm starving," barked my father.

"Elliot!"

"What? I gotta starve?"

I regret not checking the kitchen cabinet earlier. I would have let out a sigh if I possessed the organs required. I opted to put the salad in the zebra striped bowls, leaving the vagina shaped bowls on their shelf.

"Thank you, Honey!"

"Yes, thank you very much Trenton."

"It's my pleasure Ramona." I joined them at the table. "Please, tell me how you met my brother."

"We met in college. I was a freshman and he was..."

"Where is your salad?" Tyler interrupted.

"I'm not hungry, I divided it by four so you could each get more. Happy?"

"Oh Honey, here have a little of mine."

"It's okay Mom. Anyway, Ramona, you were saying?"

"I met Tyler in college, I was a freshman and he was too but he was a little different..."

"Yeah, yeah. I was older than everyone. I bet my big brother didn't even know I went to college? Did you?"

"I didn't, but that's great. I am happy for you."

"Yeah, well, I am probably a lot smarter than you now, so watch out."

"Watch out for what?"

"For me outsmarting you, that's what."

"Tyler!"

"Why would you want to outsmart me?"

"I don't know. I was kiddin.' Jesus Christ, where'd you learn to take a joke?"

"I suppose you and Dad, why?"

There would have been a long silence but luckily for our ears my father munched his salad with gusto and filled the gap with crunching sounds.

"So, Honey. Are you still driving?"

"No, they finally phased us all out last year."

"Robots?"

"Yeah, robots."

My father pounded his fist on the table.

"Fuck the robots."

Perhaps one thing we could agree on.

"It's okay. I found a better job."

"Oh Honey, great! What is it?"

"I am the superintendent of this building actually."

"It's a real shit hole."

"Tyler!"

"We're very proud of you Honey, aren't we?"

From the way my father suddenly was alert, I could tell he was kicked under the table.

"Yeah, good one."

"What is?" I questioned.

"You know, what you said. It is fine."

"What did I say?"

"What is this? Twenty Questions all of a sudden? Why do I get the interrogation? You're the one who disappeared."

"I didn't disappear."

He pounded the table again. "Well, I certainly didn't know where to find you."

"Here. I was right here."

"Well, you never called."

"You never called me!"

"What? It's my job to do everything? I gave you life isn't that enough?"

"Elliot!"

"Ouch!"

"We're very proud of you, Honey. I always knew you'd be something one day."

"Yeah, something..."

"Where'd you get such a hard-on for zebras?"

"Tyler!"

"What? Look." Tyler displayed the bowl for his wife.

"So when are you getting that food? I am starving."

"Hold on a minute."

"I've been holding on over an hour, I'm done holding on."

"Are you seeing anybody Trenton?" my mother tried to change the subject.

"Yeah, Mom. You gotta meet her. She's the prettiest woman on the whole planet."

"Oh yeah, what's her name?"

"Alberta. She's a doctor."

"My ass!"

"Tyler!"

"Well, I'd love to meet her Honey."

"You are going to love her Mom."

I held my mother's hand in mine. I truly missed her. Even now, even though she was right here.

"If you're the superintendent of this building then why is your unit a sty?"

"I rarely use this unit anymore. In fact, I try to rent it out to the people outside, make sure that some of them have a warm meal and a safe place at night."

"That's really brave of you Trenton."

"Thanks Ramona."

"I could use a warm meal myself. What the fuck?"

"Elliot!"

"Yeah, Jesus. What else do you got?"

"Tyler!"

For a second I almost believed it. All of it.

But, then I remembered the three bodies under the bed. Hell, I was dead myself.

There was no fixing anything. It was all too fucked to fix.

I only had one way to go and that was forward. I went into the kitchen.

"Hey, Trenton. C'mon. I was just kiddin'."

I took a pizza out of the oven. The extra cooking made the crust sturdy. I was able to deliver it to the table with one hand. My mother reached to take it from me.

"Ouch!"

It dropped to the table.

"I'm sorry, Mom."

"It's okay Honey. Jeez that pizza is hot."

"Yeah, sorry."

I handed Ramona a knife to cut the pizza.

"You had pizza this whole time and I'm over here chewing my fucking nails!"

I head back into the kitchen. This time, I caught my reflection in the window. It wasn't me. Year after year, walking past that window every night, catching a glimpse of myself in the darkness. But I saw something new. I was a monster. I mean I had already known it, I guess, I just had a way of not thinking about it. But here I was. Right before my very eyes. My very dead eyes.

Could I really do this? Wasn't this the ultimate crime? To kill the very people that gave me life.

I was doing this for them.

I pulled the soup out of the refrigerator and gave it a stir. There wasn't any other option so I ladled the soup into the vaginal bowls.

When I returned I saw the pizza was gone. I set the bowls of soup in front of them and set one for myself.

"Here Honey. I saved you a slice."

My mother slid her plate over to me. Something inside of me revolted, I couldn't look at her. I turned my head as far as I could from her but that meant looking at my father. I quickly averted my eyes. I stared into my soup. My reflection danced in refractions of itself. I noticed ripples in the water. Tears were falling into my soup. My soul was crying.

"What is this shit?"

My father dropped his spoon into the bowl.

"Mom, you eat the pizza please. I'll have the soup."

My father picked up the spoon and started to glug the soup again. Probably so he could complain again.

And he did.

"This soup tastes like metal, Trenton."

"No Honey, you take the pizza. I want to try your soup."

"Don't bother, Ma. Dad's right, this shit is no good."

I picked up the bowl and slurped it straight from the bowl.

"I think its fine."

"Bullshit. It tastes like a robot fucked a tomato."

"Ty…"

Ramona's plea was drowned out by my father's booming laugh. A laugh I can never recall hearing before. It shook the room.

"Fucked a tomato!" he repeated.

"No, Mom. Please. Eat the pizza."

"It's okay Honey."

I grabbed her hand, mainly to prevent her from using the spoon.

"I love you Mom."

"Well, I think your soup is terrific Trenton."

"It tastes like-ah robot fucked…" my father couldn't finish that sentence because he burst back into laughter.

"Fuck, I tried. I really did, but I can't eat this shit."

"Tyler!"

"It's true, I won't do it."

"Don't be such a baby."

Ramona picked up the bowl and chugged.

"Ramona! Stop! Ramona!"

I spun to try to stop her but Tyler shoved me back.

"Hey, Cool it!"

"Ramona, don't finish it I was hoping we'd finish at the same time. I want to course this out."

"Course? Wait. You got more food and you're making me drink this swill?"

"Tyler!"

Ramona's bowl was empty - until Tyler saw what the bowl was meant to look like. Soup squirted out of his nose and mouth filling his wife's bowl back up a bit as he laughed and gargled hysterically.

"This soup isn't so bad Honey. It's awfully rich though. Next time you should add a little wine."

"Mom. Please. You can have the pizza."

"Oh for fucksake."

My father grabbed the pizza off the plate and stuffed it in his mouth.

"Trenton, could you open a window? I'm suddenly very warm."

Tyler was still hysterical. He was trying to let us in on his little secret but for now laughter had hold of him and no matter how hard it seemed to be shaking him it wasn't letting go anytime soon.

I stood up and took my bowl and then my mother's and head for the window.

"Oh Honey. I was still working on that."

Tyler began to pound the table.

"What's so funny?" my father begged.

"Honey, I liked your soup."

"Here, have mine."

My father slid his bowl to my mother.

"Wait, Mom."

"Jesus Christ, Ty, what is so goddamn funny?"

Tyler held the bowl up, his laughter rose in pitch as he took a deep breath in. From the emphatic look his eyebrows gave, he was freeing himself from laughter.

"Cunt," he barked and fell back into the grip of laughter. My father quickly joined him.

"Tyler!"

But, nothing would snap him out of it. The only way out was to let each laugh escape. Only then could he return to normal.

Each laugh was a confirmation on every 'I wonder what my brother is doing now?' that he ever thought – and then some. Shit house. Dildo in the drawer. Bowls shaped like cunts! He probably didn't see that one coming. I knew it should be humiliating but I didn't care. I knew it wasn't true.

"Tyler!"

Ramona was no longer reprimanding her husband. She was beckoning him but he didn't notice. She had called out his name so many times he was numb to it.

"Tyler!"

Ramona clutched her husband but it was too late. She collapsed to the floor. He couldn't save her now.

"Ha. Ha. Ramona? Ha. Jesus! Ramona!"

Tyler finally snapped to it. He dropped to his wife's side; his fingers tested her neck. We waited in silence. After a few seconds his fingers delivered a message to my brother. They said: "Your wife is dead."

"What the fuck? What the fuck happened? Ramona?"

"What's going on?"

"She's not breathing, Pop! What do I do?"

"Call 9-1-1!"

"Honey, where is your phone?"

"I'll go get it."

I head back into the kitchen. I couldn't handle this.

"Ramona!"

They were frantic in there. I leaned up against the wall and visualized taking deep breaths. It wasn't as good as the real thing. I picked up the phone and dialed but then remembered the bodies and set the phone down.

"Ma! What's wrong?"

"Holly!"

I ran back into the room. My mother was coughing.

"Mom? What's wrong?"

She continued to cough and just pointed at herself coughing.

"Mom. I love you!"

My brother started coughing too.

"I'm so sorry Mom. I love you so much."

"Sorry? Ma, what the Hell is this?"

"You poisoned us!"

My mother recoiled from me. She couldn't believe it.

"I didn't poison anybody, I drank the soup too."

"He's tricking us!"

"Fuck you Trenton!"

My brother charged at me, slamming me into the wall.

"You fucking killed my wife!"

"Get off of me."

My brother sneezed in my face, the temporary loss of control allowed me to overpower him and wiggle free.

"What the fuck have you done now Trenton?"

"Dad! I didn't do anything. We need to get Mom help."

"Didn't you call…?" My brother's sentence was cut short by a few sneezes.

"They are on their way," I turned back to my mom, "Mom?"

She was dead.

"Mom?"

"You killed Mom!"

Tyler charged again but he was sneezing heavily. He was easy to push aside. He tumbled over a chair and onto the floor.

"You're a fucking monster!"

"Dad, calm down."

He didn't. Instead he picked up a chair and threw it at me. It missed, landing on the table, shattering a vagina bowl. Shards rained on my brother, my mother, and me.

"You fucking monster!"

He flipped the table over. The rest of the bowls broke. It was probably for the best. This crime scene was hideous enough without them.

"Dad. Calm down."

"You are no son of mine," he wielded another chair. "I always knew something was wrong with you."

"Dad…"

"Shut up! I ain't your dad. You're a monster. I always knew it."

He approached swinging wildly. He didn't drink enough soup. I was doomed.

"Dad, please!"

"Shut up! Shut up!"

He broke the chair over my head, driving me to my knees. I tried to get up but he had me in a submission hold. He was a master of making my brother and I submit. Fortunately, my brother was dead - and so was I. My father began to choke me with all his might. He screamed at the top of his lungs.

"Freeze!"

He was yelling too loud to hear anyone else but him.

"Freeze!"

"You are no son of mine! I'll send you back to Hell!"

I stared into my father's eyes and saw nothing but hatred. He hated me my whole life. But, in reality he knew nothing about me. He never asked. At some point he made the conscious decision to stop caring about me. Unfortunately, it was sometime before I could remember.

I never had a shot.

Each year – a wider gap grew between us. Maybe he didn't hate me? Maybe he hated himself? I don't know. My brother was a second chance for him to become a father. To his credit he ended up doing pretty good.

"Freeze!"

I didn't know where the hate in my father's eyes came from, but I saw it in there. It was impossible to not see. Years growing apart only to run towards this evening from our opposite sides, clashing. I could feel this. I could feel this in my soul. I couldn't feel my father choking me but what I felt was probably a lot worse. It felt like anxiety, a chilly paralysis, holding me down like it had my whole life. I was frozen in the same old nightmare.

"Freeze!"

The anxiety trapped me. It was only fitting my father was holding me down - like he always had - physically or otherwise.

I stared into my father's eyes until they exploded along with the rest of his head. He slumped off me and I climbed to my feet. The immense anxiety was no more. I finally woke up from that nightmare.

I was free.

"Are you okay, Sir?" A policeman stood with his gun smoking.

"Thank you," I sobbed. "He was on a rampage. You saved me."

"Sir, please get down. Sir, please step back."

I approached him quickly.

"Is this your normal beat?"

"Sir, stop or I will have to shoot!"

"Do you recognize this place?"

He backed away defensively, hoping to maintain some space.

"Get down! This is your last warning!"

"Were you the asshole who stole my fucking ice trays?"

He fired a few shots into me but it was no use. I was just as disappointed as he was to find out that bullets weren't going to put me out of my misery.

I swiped a broken piece of cunt off the ground and cut the policeman's neck. He staggered backwards and died.

I tried to remove the policeman's gun but I couldn't undo the strap, so instead I took off his entire belt.

"Get down on your knees, asshole!" yelled his partner.

I disobeyed. He tried to stop me, firing three bullets into my chest, but it didn't matter much.

Now that I was wearing the belt I had the proper leverage to unholster the gun. I looked at it as he fired a fourth bullet.

"No safety, huh?"

"You're under arrest."

"Not anymore."

I shot him dead.

The room was nothing but death and broken bullshit.

I admired the gun in my hands. It sure was a lot easier killing with one of these things.

22.

Flies occasionally flew out of my shirt collar. I pulled up my shirt to investigate and noticed my wound was providing shelter to a few dozen maggots. I stood watching them squirm. In a way, I didn't mind. It was nice to have some life in me – no matter how disgusting it might be.

My shirt was somehow grosser than the rest of me. The deaths of nine people evidently made their mark on my clothing. Dried blood resembled spilt wine. I probably looked like a wino, which all things considered is a pretty nice disguise.

I pulled my list out and crossed off the top of it:
~~Parents.~~

"Who's next?"

Most of these people were going to require a lot of effort to find. In fact, I only knew where I could find two of them – Eugene Page and Linn Ochoco.

I decided on Linn Ochoco.

I picked her for three main reasons. One, she was the closest. Two, I wasn't eager to see Sherman Caruthers or any of his inventions just yet. Three, Linn is an older woman; she should be a lot easier to kill.

After last night - easy sounds ideal.

Linn Ochoco's business empire and warehouses surrounded the intersection of Alameda and Clock streets - about two miles from here. I started east.

6th Street used to be the main artery of Skid Row in Los Angeles. Now pretty much all of downtown was Skid Row. Someone stabbed this city in the heart and the blood never stopped gushing.

I'll never understand why Los Angeles allowed Skid Row in the first place. Granted, I didn't know what other big cities were like, but I doubted they'd forfeit half of their downtown to create a tent city where drugs and mental illness are allowed to run various experiments on the human mind.

Rumor has it: as soon as other cities caught wind of Skid Row, they dumped their collections of crazies and craziers off onto 6th by the busload. Los Angeles already had the reputation for being a crazy magnet – fame attracts most the worst minds from all over the country. The injustice of Skid Row quickly made sure it got all the rest of them, including the ones who didn't know where or what a Los Angeles was.

A bank clock notified me it was 106 degrees out. Just a few degrees cooler and the streets would likely be chaos. When the heat flared up – so did the people. Currently it was too hot. Too hot to be agitated – too hot for anything.

"Hey, can I have your sweater?"

He was either dead or asleep. I stepped on the man's heel to rouse him.

"Hey, it's awful hot out, don't you think? I'll trade you for your sweater."

"Huh?"

"Give me your sweater," I tried to pull it off of him.

"Why?"

"It's too hot, you should take it off."

"Then what you want it for?"

"I want it for this." I took the baton out of the dead policeman's belt. "A baton."

The homeless man flinched away from me. I could see a giant scar running along the entirety of his head. I set the baton on his lap. He grabbed it and swung defensively. I backed away.

"Alright, now give me the sweater."

He pulled the sweater off and threw it at me. The baton was back in his hands.

"Thanks."

"Baton Rouge," he yelled.

"Same to you, Buddy."

The homeless man's baggy sweater was covered in unique snowflakes of dried crud. It was no better looking than my current clothes but at least it would hide all the blood. I pulled it over and walked away.

I noticed Immigreat Incorporated from a mile away. It was the last hair standing on this balding part of the city. The complex was massive. However, unlike Caruthers' Innovations, this campus sprawled upward not outward. There weren't giant lawns to beautify anything. All the space was for something. Everything here served a purpose.

There was one giant security gate. It was the only way in or out. Some companies had walls like these to keep the workers in. Not these. These were legitimate and clearly around for protection. The vacant lot across the street was swarming with vagrants.

I cross the street and join them. I blend in pretty well over here.

Everyone on this side was lying around. It was too hot to do anything else. I was the only one in the field sitting upright. I watched the gate with much interest. Not only for Linn but the comings and goings of everyone else. Immigreat was busy. Busy with real humans. I didn't see a single robot in the entire bunch. Human security, human drivers, human everything.

I looked behind me at all the melting American men. They had nothing to do.

I noticed Linn Ochoco right away. Not from her looks, she was rather plain and wore very humble clothes, but from how everyone acted when she walked by. They were practically bowing. She was like a Saint.

After a long series of 'thank yous' and 'goodbyes' Linn Ochoco walked up Alameda. She was with a woman and a man in a cowboy hat. I gave them a few minutes head start and got up and walked after them.

The woman was the first to depart their trio. She stayed back at the bus stop on the corner of 6th and Alameda.

Linn Ochoco was more than a celebrity at her work. People passing by on the streets recognized her; some highly regarded her, and a few seemed to worship her. She stopped to hug and talk to so many people that I had pretty much caught up to them. I bent over and pretended to tie my shoes to buy myself some time.

I noticed a splatter of blood on my shoes. I licked my thumb instinctively before trying to wipe it off but I couldn't seem to get my thumb wet. Linn was still busy chatting so I scratched off the blood with my fingernail.

I let her get a lot further ahead this time, which was good because she got stopped at least twice a block. I had never seen someone get so much attention. When I was alive I had a hard enough time to get someone to look me in the eyes. I don't think anyone ever crossed a street to hug me my entire life. So far, Linn Ochoco, has had five people do it.

The abandoned warehouses along Alameda weren't much to look at but they provided a lot of shade. Hundreds of people huddled up with their backs against the wall. For the people on the eastside of the street, their shade was waning. You could tell by the way they all sat with their knees tucked under their armpits.

After 3rd there wasn't much around. It used to be Little Tokyo, but the Japanese moved west, where it was nicer. Now this area was either open fields or empty brick buildings made up to look like Japan. Linn Ochoco and her cowboy friend walked at a faster pace now.

There wasn't anyone around to interrupt them and for good reason. There was no shade over here. The sun was screaming down on all of us. I saw my sweater was damp, especially around my stomach.

I thought about shooting them both from here but there was nowhere to escape if the cops saw or heard me do it. I figured I'd keep following them. So far I was better at winging it than coming up with any plans.

The exposé on Linn Ochoco from *Humans Magazine* wasn't exaggerating. Despite owning an empire she really took the subway.

I followed her inside of Union Station. A mural above the door caught my attention. Ten faces – young and old, men and women, and seemingly of every ethnicity looked down at me. Their lips were painted with disappointment. Not only at me, but I guess for anyone who walked in here.

Linn and her cowboy friend got in the queue. I waited for it to fill up a bit before I merged in. We slowly snaked forward. Everyone presented a card and tapped the palm of a giant robot. Our progress came to a halt anytime one of the robots had to deal with a cardless person, casting them aside with a scoop. As we got closer I saw the robots were scanning the people as they tapped. I wasn't sure what was going to happen to me but I didn't think any harm could come from trying.

Literally. I don't think anything is going to hurt me at this point.

When it was my turn the machine tried to scan but it didn't seem to register. I walked through and nothing happened.

"Hey!"

I turned around and saw the man behind me was complaining.

"Hey! He just walked through."

The robot seemed to hear him but it couldn't do anything. It was programmed to do two things and that didn't include fixing any of its errors.

Once the annoying man was on my side of security he came at me.

"Hey! I saw you. You didn't pay."

"Would you shut up about it? The robot didn't care. Why should you?"

"The robot did care!"

"Whose side are you on? The humans or the robots?"

"I'm on nobody's side!"

We were drawing an audience. I saw Linn's friend's hat in the distance. They were getting away.

"Good. Then leave me alone."

"No! You cheated."

"Fuck you, asshole. Cheated who? The robot? Are you upset because you didn't get to come in for free too?"

"No fuck you!"

I thought about shooting him but showing him the gun was enough.

"Quiet down, asshole! I'm undercover, all right? Now buzz off!"

He did as he was commanded. I took off after Linn. I followed the signs for the subway. After I descended another set of stairs I saw the cowboy hat and honed in. But, when I reached him, he was alone. I spiraled out from him hoping she was nearby but I didn't see her anywhere.

I should have killed her earlier.

"Where is Linn?"

"¿Que?"

"¿Donde es Linn Ochoco?"

"Morado," he pointed up. This was the gold line.

I saw a sign for the purple line and exited without a goodbye or adios.

Linn Ochoco was at the end of the platform, shaking hands with a young couple. They all seemed to be laughing. I clonked down the stairs and head straight for them.

Union Station was nicer than most stations but it still suffered from the same problems that cursed them all: stale air, no where to sit, and the same gloomy smear of fuck that has gathered on the far wall of the station. Luckily every ten minutes a subway hides that dirty wall. The same ten minutes that makes cleaning that wall impossible without losing a few dozen humans or robots in the process.

The monitor above displayed that the purple line would arrive in three minutes - enough time for me to shoot Linn and board the subway. I pulled the gun out and charged forward.

"Aguas!"

She saw me coming. Despite my mangled face, despite the gun in my hand, she didn't flinch when I started shooting at her.

"Señora!"

Linn Ochoco was a woman of the people. They loved her. From what I could tell it was for good reason. She was humble; she was strong. I understood why someone would cross a street to hug her.

But, taking a bullet for her. It floored me.

Actually, Linn Ochoco floored me.

I was frozen with envy. I couldn't react in time. She leapt over her injured saviors and tackled me. The gun fired once in my hand but then she had it. She beat me over the head with it, shoving my mess under my nose like you would shame a bad dog. I tried for the gun but she threw it off the platform.

She grabbed my arms and beat the sides of my head with them. She was yelling something to the crowd but I couldn't hear over my beating. When the crowd joined in on the stomping I figured out what she must have said to them.

I couldn't feel their blows but they kept me down all the same. I tried to get to my feet but they'd kick me back to the ground. I didn't give up, eventually I scared them with my relentlessness or they were getting tired. Either way, the crowd lightened up a bit. I was able to regain my ground. They backed away from me.

"He's a monster!"

I roared and beat my chest. They backed up further. I tried to play it up.

"Linn Ochoco," I pointed at her. "I have come here to kill you."

Despite having the stature of a summer squash, Linn Ochoco moved like a jungle cat. She had the ferocity of one too. She surged from the crowd and came straight at me again. She hit me with two jabs then I don't know what happened but I was on the ground again. She tried to mount me but I kicked her off.

Her hair flowed around her – she looked possessed. It was wind. The subway was coming.

I looked down at the tracks but I couldn't see the gun. I was going to have to try something else. I pulled up the sweater and examined the contents of the police belt.

I regretted trading that baton.

I stood up and the subway rushed by.

The crowd ran for the front of the platform. Away from me. The subway stopped and they started disappearing inside. Linn Ochoco slowly backed away from me; she was still surrounded by a posse. She was getting away.

"Linn Ochoco! I have come here to kill you!"

She was a fighter. She showed that much. My last chance was to appeal to that nature. As I walked towards her, I gestured my palm. "Come at me," it said.

It worked.

"Linn! No!"

"Vamos señora."

But she didn't listen. She meant to put an end to this.

I preemptively blocked my face and she took the bait. She sent a right hook right into my stomach. Her fist plowed into nothing but cotton. I grabbed her other wrist and applied handcuffs.

"I want you to know I am doing this for your own good."

I slapped the other ratchet onto a handrail on the back of the subway car.

"Please stand clear – the doors are closing."

Linn Ochoco's posse switched into high gear. But, no matter how many of them banged on the subway, no matter how many of them pulled on that rail, no matter how many of them clawed at Linn's arms – they could not save her.

The robot subway-driver wasn't programmed for a scenario like this, so it reacted the same way it reacted to everything. It closed the doors and punched ahead. They didn't call it the 'next stop' for nothing.

The subway's acceleration yanked Linn Ochoco down into the depths of Los Angeles, bouncing her violently off each wooden plank until it gained enough speed that she resembled a flag in the wind.

Just like that - she was gone.

The posse stared down the tunnel, their jaws showcasing their disbelief. I slowly backed away but then they all turned. All eyes on me.

"What have you done?"

"You're a murderer!"

"A monster!"

I pulled a canister of mace out from the police belt and gave it a shake.

"Clacka-clacka-clacka," replied the can of mace.

The sound caused laughter to erupt from within me. I remembered the rat-faced man.

He was right after all.

I sprayed at the dead woman's posse like they were cockroaches on a kitchen counter. They scattered.

Now, I was alone on the platform. I hopped down on the tracks and picked up the gun and put it in its holster. Then I climbed back up.

I leaned up against a pillar and waited for the next train.

23.

"Jesus, Man. Did something crawl down your throat and die?"

"Can I tell you a secret?"

"Phew, sure, as long as you tell it, facing the other way."

I turned my head and obliged. I hadn't given my breath much thought but I suppose it was as foul as breath could get.

"Alright, well, it's more of a show than a tell. Ready?"

I looked back at him and he gave me a nod. I pulled up the sweater and bloody shirt and showed the man, no, nothing crawled down my throat, but this is as close as it gets.

He puked right into my lap, some of it splashed into my opening. Flies buzzed out of me.

"Aww, c'mon!"

The man tried to speak but he threw up again. He staggered away, leaving a trail of vomit in the direction he went. The park bench was mine.

I picked up his newspaper and read through it. I felt like I read it before. The news is always the same, only the names and dates change. I turned to 'the funnies' and was a little more entertained. In a way I find the comics the most impressive part of a newspaper. It's the only section that is obligated to be different everyday.

An ad on the back of the paper caught my attention. It said: "Star Maps". Underneath that, there was a list of intersections. 3rd and Fairfax was a bit up the street. So I started walking.

The closer I got to the Farmer's Market, the more tourists I encountered. Each one of them gave me a bad look, whether sadness or anger, it was all negative. This haggard look may be commonplace on the eastside but over here I stood out like a sore thumb.

"Star maps here!"

"Can I take a look at that real quick?"

"Sure, $5 then you can do whatever you want with it."

He ashed his cigar on the milk crate between his legs and let out a laugh. I squat down on his level.

"I'll trade you this newspaper for a map. I need to take a peak."

"I don't care what you need to take. I only need to take money, get me?"

"Please, Sir, I will give it back."

"Good, pretend you already did."

"Sir…"

"You're startin' to get on my nerves!"

I stood back up and took a step forward so that I would be towering over him.

"Just hand me a fucking map or else."

"Or else what?"

I lifted up my shirt and thrust it right in his face. He banged the back of his head against the wall and then recoiled off the milk crate. I took a map and opened it up.

"Let's see here…" Jesus Christ… "There's no way, when were these printed?"

I looked back at the Star Map Man but he was halfway up the block, frantically crabwalking away. I flipped the map over and saw the date was current.

"My, how the mighty have fallen."

24.

Thai Town was a Hell of a place for anyone to live, let alone a famous Hollywood actor like Umatilla Harney. Alberta grew up watching him. I grew up watching him. Everyone must have – he was in everything. But, I guess it didn't add up to as much as it seemed. Otherwise it did and he was lousy with it.

Umatilla lived on a small stretch of Russell Boulevard that only existed for two blocks. It was a real skidmark of a street. His wild unattended yard obscured the façade of his pastel bungalow. It looked like a rotten Easter egg nobody ever found.

Shockingly, I could see him upstairs. His curtains were drawn. His bedroom window was like a television, displaying Umatilla Harney in his saddest role to date – Today.

He disappeared off camera. I took that as my cue to get closer. I snuck through a part in his fence that was missing the most pickets. I saw him come down the stairs and go into the kitchen. I tried the front door but it was locked. The garage however, was unlocked. I opened it a bit and rolled in.

Inside the garage was a lime green 1970 Lamborghini Miura. I was glad to see that Mr. Harney held on to at least some of his wealth.

I poked my head inside the car. The steering wheel had an image of a golden bull on it. I touched it with my finger at the same time I heard a slamming sound, then the garage door sprang to life.

I hid the only place I could – under the car.

I immediately regretted it. I should have struck while the iron was hot as they say. Instead, Umatilla Harney got in the car and started it up. It started rolling away so I did the only think I could think of – I held on.

Once we were in the driveway he pulled the emergency brake. Now was my chance. I just had to club him over the head and drag him back to the garage.

Unfortunately, Mr. Harney's garage routine was years in the making - he was back in the car before I was out from under it. I rolled back and held on for dear life, or dear death. I grabbed the wrong way. It worked for the rest of our reversal, but when he pulled forward the car spun me around and drove over my back legs.

Our pace on Russell was encouraging but by the time Harney took a left on Western he really opened up the engine. My shoes dragged along beneath me, after a few blocks I saw smoke start to come off my heels.

At red lights I'd try to survey the damage but I could never get a good view without letting go of the car's undercarriage.

"Hey Mr. Harney, how ya doing today?"

"Today's a good day to die," laughed Umatilla Harney.

He was right.

A series of metal strips dug into my back as the car lurched forward. We drove at a slow pace until we parked.

Again, Harney was out before I could react. I rolled from under the car and watched him jog off. I looked around - I was on a real Hollywood set. An alien walked by and waved at me. I waved back and took off after Harney.

I kept my distance as we weaved through a series of non-descript buildings. He pulled into one marked 6-A. I waited a few seconds and went in after him.

The studio lot looked like they did in the movies, which now that I thought about it, wasn't all the impressive considering all they had to do was turn the camera around or back it up a little.

A series of director's chairs were splayed in front of the lit backdrops. Despite all the wonderful colors on stage my eyes were focused on one thing and one thing only - the name on the back of the third chair from the left.

Brooklyn Kelly

"Hey, what're you doing?"

I turned around and a man wearing a headset was pointing at me.

"Yeah, you. What're you doing?"

"I'm an extra."

"What the Hell are you supposed to be?"

"I'm a corpse."

"Not in this picture, you ain't."

He grabbed me by the back of the arm and led me
through a hallway behind the set. It fed us back
outside.

"Stay back here. I'll figure out what the Hell is going
on."

As soon as the man went back inside, I took off.

The studio was chaos. People drove every which way
on every which vehicle. Men peddled by on bikes. A
woman zoomed in a golf cart. A young actress on a
Segway leaned her way forward.

I flagged down a man driving a forklift.

"Hey, Buddy. Do you know where I could find the
stars' dressing rooms?"

"Sure, hop on."

"Thanks."

I sat down next to him.

"Jeez, take a look at you. You look like the real
deal."

"Yeah, I can still hardly believe it myself."

I was surprised to see that the stars' area was nothing
but a glorified trailer park. Rows of equally spaced
trailers line the parking lot behind the non-descript
buildings.

"This is your stop."

I hopped out of the forklift and he took off.

There were three rows of trailers, each capped off at the end with a larger trailer, forming cul-de-sacs. I walked down the first row and knocked on the door of the largest trailer.

There was no answer.

Or lock.

I stepped inside and was surprised at how spacious the interior was - enough to fit two couches. I looked at the mail on the coffee table and saw this was the trailer for Rex Malden. I didn't know who he was. But, I saw he had knives in the kitchen and that was good enough. I took the biggest one out of the knife block.

Thanks Rex.

I needed a place to hide it so I jammed it into my upper thigh and pulled the sweater to conceal the handle. I was a glorified pincushion. Before leaving, I grabbed a bottle of mouthwash off the counter and chugged it.

By the time I was out the door, the mouthwash started leaking out of me. The flies weren't having it. A half-dozen flew out from my collar.

"Ingrates."

I walked down the next aisle of trailers and tried the door of the largest trailer at the end.

This one had a lock.

And somebody inside.

I heard some scratching on the wall and then the blinds shot open, revealing the scowl of Umatilla Harney.

"What the Hell do you want?"

"Hello Sir. Do you know where Brooklyn Kelly is?"

The blinds shut as quickly as they opened. There was silence. I paused for a response but after a few minutes I realized there was none.

I knocked.

"Goddammit!" I heard Umatilla Harney yell through the wall.

This time he opened the door.

For an old man he sure was tall. Granted, he was at the top of a staircase. Up close his tan skin looked like he was fried, not by the Hollywood sun but by hot oil. He looked like an onion ring.

"What the Hell are you supposed to be?"

"I'm a zombie."

"Well, get the fuck out of here. I don't care."

He stepped back and reached for the door.

"Wait. Do you know where Brooklyn Kelly is?"

"Oh, would you like me to take you to her?"

He opened the door. Only so he could slam it.

"Too bad! Now get the fuck outta here."

"I'll be back," I promised.

I head for the third and final row of the trailers. I head for the one at the end and gave it a knock.

I waited for a spell but there was no movement inside. I twisted the knob and it gave free, it was unlocked. I stepped inside.

Unlike the first trailer, this one was very personalized. A heart shaped bed took up the center of the trailer. Above the bed hung a painting of cupid, bow poised. The walls were lined with racks of wardrobes.

I walked around the bed and towards the kitchen. The trailer clearly is intended for a woman but I still need evidence it belongs to Brooklyn. Something like...

Brooklyn herself.

"Hey, what're you doing in here?"

She exited a bathroom and came right at me. Her finger pushed me towards the kitchen counter. Her finger said: "we aren't afraid of the likes of you."

"I'm sorry to barge in here Ms. Kelly. Really I am..."

"Well, then do me a favor and get out of here," she interrupted.

"I am sure you get this a lot but I am one of your biggest fans. I came here because I have something important..."

"Good. Write it down and put it in the mail."

With that, she forced me toward the exit. I stumbled over the heart shaped bed and fell on top of it.

"I wish I had my copy of *Wild Roses* with me but I think the cops took it. Listen, I know this sounds crazy, but is it possible to give you a kiss?"

"First, get off my bed," she stared at me until I obeyed her command. "Second, how about you come back without that horrifying costume and I'll reconsider depending on how handsome you are. Also, do me a favor - take a bath. You smell like a mint-flavored orangutan."

"This isn't a costume. This is my real face."

"Well, I hope your mother kept your receipt."

"My mother is dead."

"Listen dickhead, my statements aren't an extention of any conversation. They are social cues that are telling you to get the fuck out of my trailer. Got it?"

She was so fierce. A lifetime playing damsels in distress - she had me fooled. She was a better actress than I ever thought.

Brooklyn Kelly aged beautifully too. She didn't hide her flaws with collagen or surgery - she embraced them. The lines in her face showed a life of laughing and smiling. Her beauty was in her personification of joy.

"Did you hear me?"

"You're so beautiful."

"That's it."

Brooklyn jumped over the bed and stormed me, raining down a series of fists and kicks. I stumbled back but held my ground, grabbing her wrist; we struggled.

"Get out, goddammit."

Her face began to redden. Our wriggling caused her to perspire. Drops of sweat begin to appear along her blonde hairline and cascade down her cheek, filling the ravines of her past joy with the anguish of now.

She bit my shoulder, hoping to relax my grip but it only allowed me to nuzzle her neck. I ran my nose along her skin like a paintbrush. If only I could smell this moment.

I imagined her skin smelling of honey and butter. The room probably smelled of flowers and expensive Parisian perfume.

Brooklyn jerked her head away from mine and locked eyes with me. I saw the terror in them, but it wasn't the embellished kind I had seen from her in the movies. This fear looked glazed over. Tired.

She gave out a groan and I met her lips with mine. Her low hum resonated in the hollows on my head. Our kiss created an echo chamber.

I hauled her over to the heart shaped bed and her grip and weight pulled me down with her. I fell in-between her legs and deepened the kiss. She cried out and I bored my tongue into hers.

"Please…"

The juices of her tongue moistened mine. It went from rigid to flexible again in moments.

Brooklyn clawed at my waist. Her hand found the handle of my hidden knife. She tried to free it from my pants but I tore her hand free and unsheathed it myself.

"Please…"

I plunged the shaft deep into her. Her eyes watered and she writhed but she made no sounds besides her heavy panting. The opening gushed hot blood, pooling on her polyester dress and down my pants. It dripped all the way down to the floor.

Brooklyn tried to speak but her words spilled out of her abdomen instead of her mouth. My hand left the shaft and brushed her face. I held out a solitary finger and held it over her luscious lips. My finger said: "Quiet, save your words."

Until she bit it off.

I stuck the blade deeper and she gave out a cough, causing her teeth to lose control of my finger. It lodged itself in her throat. Her eyes grew wide and she gagged.

"I'm sorry Brooklyn. You'll never know how much I loved you."

She turned away from me, choking.
It wasn't until I pushed the knife deeper that she returned eye contact.

She was dead.

I had imagined sharing a bed with this woman my entire life and now I was, although, suffice to say, this wasn't quite the scene I had wanted. I had dreamt of something romantic but this reality was perverse.

She was dead. I was dead. There was always the afterlife.

We could start again fresh.

I took the finger out of her mouth and replaced it with my tongue.

25.

There was no answer so I pounded this time.

"Fucking Hell!"

The blinds shot open, revealing the familiar scowl of Umatilla Harney.

"You again?"

"I told you I'd be back you old asshole."

He disappeared; I wasn't sure if he heard me, but then he quickly emerged from his front door.

Before I could react I realized I was looking at him upside down and then right side up again. He kicked me down the stairs. Shortly after that he was on top of me, pummeling.

I think he heard me. That or he was angrier than I gave him credit for. Either way he was certainly taking it out on me.

Umatilla Harney's face was twisting between crying and snarling. There was madness in his eyes, a rage unrelated to me. I took his beating. I turned the other cheek and he made sure to tenderize it equally.

His deep fried skin cracked under his shirt. His armpits became damp. The moist silk looked like greasy, caramelized onions.

I wasn't aware until he was pulled off of me that our little scuffle had gathered quite an audience. Gawking men and women held their cellphones up at our scene.

"Get off of me!" Umatilla Harney howled at the two hulking teamsters that stripped him away.

I got to my feet.

"Hey, Mister!"

"Tell us what happened."

"Yeah."

"Listen," I motioned for them to calm down. "Umatilla Harney is an old asshole."

I walked away.

I could kill him and in a completely different kind of way he deserves it, but no - I'll spare him.

For Alberta's sake.

Whatever demons were haunting Umatilla Harney, they had their claws in deep. They'd fly him straight to Hell.

If he was going to have any shot at Heaven, he was going to need a lot more time down here to sort things out.

I walked up the stairs to his trailer and shut the door behind me. In comparison to the last two trailers – this one was a mess. Every flat surface held an ashtray, each with a veritable pyramid of cigarette butts.

I opened the closet and took out the nicest thing that would fit me. I kept the gun and taser from the police belt but ditched the rest, and then I peeled off my clothes, literally. I took the list out of my pocket and discarded the clothes in a heap on the floor.

A swarm of flies plummeted out of me when I was naked. They buzzed around the room, creating a static fog, like when I was a kid and my TV was on a channel that didn't exist.

I swatted at them with my bloody shirt. The flies darted and hung in the corners of the trailer and watched me leave with Umatilla Harney's car keys.

26.

I snapped the Lamborghini into fifth gear and the world around me became a blur. The road, the cars, all of it; the only constant was the dashboard. It said I was going 130 MPH.

The fact that I couldn't feel the wind blow through my hair was only a bummer until I caught my reflection in the rearview mirror. My formerly attached-by-staples scalp had been lost in the wind.

It was surprising how ugly I could keep getting. Right when I thought I reached maximum levels of repugnance I'd crash through another glass ceiling. My exposed skull looked like I was wearing a swimmer's cap that was a couple of sizes too small for my head. The loose skin around my temples flapped like reverse sideburns.

The Miura continued to missile down PCH. The cars in my rearview mirror disintegrated into the horizon. I saw a sign advertising food or something but I went by too quickly – I didn't have enough time to read it.

Cutting through the wind at that speed caused a deafening noise. Yet, somehow I was able to hear that the Miura's engine was crying. But, it didn't last long and either did the wind.

It wasn't the fact that the car broke down that scared me but where it broke down – right in front of a church.

It had to be a sign.

Or I ran out of gas.

In any case, The Miura wouldn't start back up. I was stuck here.

The wind picked up the dry sand and blew it away. I stared at the ground and watched layer after layer of sand disappear. I wondered if I stayed here long enough: would the wind eventually blow everything away?

I exited The Miura and walked across the loose Earth until I reached the wooden stairs of the church. Time and visitors alike wore away the white paint until only specks of it remained.

I worked off a strip of paint with my heel and then stepped inside.

Despite being located in the exact middle of nowhere, the church was pristine from floor to ceiling. Gold dripped from everything. It seemed the only reason there was a ring of balconies above was to have more surface area for gold to drip from.

There were dozens of pews but there was no one inside.

I tried to fake cough but couldn't muster the reflexes necessary. Instead I said the word: "cough" very loudly.

"Oh Hello there. Welcome! Please come forward."

A greying man wearing a bright red robe came out from a door on the stage. From a distance he looked like a molding bell pepper.

I wondered if he always walked around in that robe. It seemed fine in a church but anywhere else in and he'd look like a freak show, like a royal time traveler.

"Lord In Heaven! Are you alright?"

"Oh, I've been better."

"You look hurt."

"I look bad. I don't feel a thing. That's all."

"Well, good. Good to hear. What brought you here today? Would you like to confess your sins?"

"Oh, um, I am not so sure, or I don't know."

I remember Loki saying religion was bullshit but this all seemed too coincidental.

I got to my knees and prayed.

"Lord, please, I don't know what to do. Did you send me here on purpose? I don't mean to be so doubtful but could you send me another sign?"

"What's that Lord? Yes, yes, of course," the pepper colored preacher got to his knees, joining me. "I will help this man. God Bless You."

The preacher brought both of us back to a standing position. He had his arm around me.

"Did you hear that?" he asked.

"Hear what?"

"Our Lord God was just speaking to us."

"I didn't hear anything."

"You must truly be lost. But, fear not, the Lord has just proved that you are still worthy, you are to be saved. Come."

I followed the preacher up the stage and into the door I saw him emerge from. We entered his office. It was as gold as the rest of the place.

"Wait, so do you hear God all the time?"

"No, actually that was the first time. I believe it is a miracle."

"You don't seem very surprised. I mean, you've been at this a while, didn't you have anything you wanted to ask him?"

"Who am I to question God? I only do as he says."

"Well, I think it is kind of odd is all."

"What do you mean?"

"You didn't have anything to say to him? Don't you think anyone else might be interested in asking him something?"

"Never mind it, now sit down."

He pointed at one of the small leather chairs facing his desk. He got behind the desk and sat in a chair that resembled a throne.

"Hold on. How can you be so calm?"

"Take it easy, please, sit down."

"Look, I am going to come out and say it. I think you are lying."

"How dare you."

"I mean you've been practicing this for how long?"

"My whole life."

"Your whole life!" I could almost laugh, "and you don't seem any more excited than I am…"

"We didn't come in here to talk about me," he interrupted.

"I'm trying to have a conversation here."

"So am I, albeit a very different one. I am trying to save your soul here."

I sat down.

"Look, I am sorry for calling you a liar."

"It's forgiven my son."

"You of all people should believe me, so here it goes. I am dead." I lifted my shirt to prove it.

A cloud of flies birthed out of me. They flew towards the preacher but he didn't swat at them.

"Good Lord!"

"That's the thing…" I put my shirt back on. "I died and I went to Heaven. But, it isn't what you think it is, or at least, it wasn't what I thought it was supposed to be."

"You have seen God?"

"No, that's the thing. He wasn't around, apparently he has newer, more interesting places to worry about."

"Tell me, what is Heaven like."

"It was pretty shitty to be honest - dirty and broken down. It was kind of like a ghetto. It was all public housing."
"No clouds?"

"Maybe, the buildings were too tall."

"Are you sure it was Heaven you were seeing?"

"Yeah I am pretty sure."

"But, God wasn't around?"

"Yeah he was gone and from the sounds of it, he doesn't drop by that often either."

"I see."

"Well, I hope you do, because if you really did talk to him back there then I really have to ask him something."

"You are sure you are dead?"

I lift my shirt again. More flies.

"Pretty sure."

"Yes, well..." the preacher looked around nervously, "I may have heard that voice in my head, I can't be too sure."

"What is with you and being sure?"

"Don't raise your voice at me, I am trying to help."

"It doesn't matter. Can you try to get God to, I don't know, get on the line?" I imitated a telephone with my fingers.

"If only it were that easy my son."

"Well, isn't it? Don't you just do this?" I clasped my hands together in a prayer.
"I am afraid not. There are steps one must take before getting close enough to God that you can understand what he wants of you."

"I probably don't have enough time. Can you ask him for me?"

"Again, it isn't that easy…"

"Jesus, with 'easy' now, you sure get stuck on words."

"Excuse me?"

"Look, in your, holy opinion, do you think someone would ever be justified in killing?"

"Lord no! Look, it is one of the top commandments. His pointed started at the top but slowly descended down the list, towards the bottom."

"That says seven doesn't it."

"Well, yes, but it is in the top ten."

"Do the other commandments that come before it mean more?"

He turned to review them.

"Yes. I would say so."

I noticed number six. Thou shall honour thy father and thy mother. I looked away.

"Can you please get God on the line?"

"Our Lord cannot be summoned. He is not a genie."

"Please, can you try? Humor me."

"Lord, who art thou in Heaven, it is I, your faithful servant…"

"Hello?" a voice boomed inside the sanctuary.

The preacher and I jumped out of our chairs. I followed him out of the exit. A man dressed in an all white suit and white cowboy hat walked down the aisle towards us.

"That your car out front?" he asked.

"Is that God?" I asked.

"No, that's just Ivon."

Ivon walked up the stairs and extended his hand for a shake. I met it with my own.

"The name's Ivon Springwater, pleased to meet you."

"My name is Trenton. Trenton Ankeny."

"Say Cooper, that isn't your car out front is it?"

"No Sir, what car?"

"That was a joke Cooper."

"The car is mine, Sir."

"Sweet Jesus that is a fine car. Do you suppose I could take a peak inside?"

"We were kind of in the middle of something important," I replied.

"You may want to step into the office Ivon. He isn't kidding."

"Fine, fine. Let's take a look at the car; I won't need long, just a minute. Then we can get to whatever it is you boys are talking about."

"Ivon..."

"Nonsense, follow me."

The preacher looked at me and shrugged.

"He owns this place."

"Owns?" I asked.

But, The preacher didn't elaborate. Instead he sulked after his boss. I followed close behind.

"Oh wow. That is quite a car!"

"Forgive him, he's a dolt" Ivon slapped my shoulder and then pulled me with him. "Now let's take a look under her skirt, huh?"

"What?"

"Will you pop the hood please?"

"Ivon, this car is nice and all but..."

"Say! Take a look at this! It has a V12 for Christ's sake!"

"Uh, yeah I guess it does."

"I bet this thing is faster than Hell. I have a few beauties myself but I don't have a V12, that's for sure."

"Ivon, what this man has to say is more impressive than a car."

"Don't be such a hassle, Cooper. I just wanted to see the car was all," Ivon stepped away and came to shake my hand again. "You must want to make a donation."

"Excuse me?"

Ivon looked at the preacher for help, then turned back to me.

"No? What's this all about then?"

"Well, my car died out front. I thought it was a sign. I am starting to doubt it was."

Ivon turned back to his preacher.

"This isn't about money?"

"You mentioned some cars, do you happen to have any gas?" I asked.

"I'm afraid not, there is a station a few miles North."

"Is there a way I could get a ride, I am not in the best of health."

"I am afraid I am rather busy at the moment, but I always have time to talk money, perhaps we can negotiate…"

"Trenton, will you show him what you showed me in the office."

"No I think this was all a mistake."

"Listen, a Top Banana like you can spare a little coin," Ivon Springwater rubbed his finger and thumb together on my lapel to judge the quality. "You see, I have gas and want money but I don't have the time. You have money and want time but don't have the gas. We can help each other. Trenton, was it?"

"If that is how it's going to be, all right. Where is your car?"

"Trenton!" the preacher stomped.

"Aww, quiet down Cooper."

"Lead the way."

27.

Ivon Springwater's car was nice but compared to the Miura it was quite slow. But, it had gas and I suppose that is all that matters.

It was smooth sailing until I reached Mid City; traffic plugged the way so I exited on La Brea and head north.

La Brea meant The Tar. Los Angeles was covered in it, a jumble of streets plowing right through one another. So many streets and so many names but few were as fitting as La Brea.

In fact, Los Angeles should really be called La Brea.

The city's veins and arteries were made of la brea before they were paved with it. The tar oozed out of Los Angeles like pus for millions of years. Later they fenced off the area and made it a tourist attraction – The La Brea Tar Pits (translation: The The Tar Tar Pits).

Before a city was here, that pit swallowed a vast collection of Earth's living history, from sabre-toothed tigers to the American lion, from snail to mammoth.

La Brea, a festering boil, arguably dead center in LA County has pulled in victims for millions of years. Cries of the powerless lured predators to come capitalize. Only to then become stuck themselves; a steady string of animals biting each other on the ass and dragging each other to the pits of Hell.

In a lot of ways, things haven't changed.

On my left, I saw a large queue formed; it was leading to a hotdog stand – Pink's. I pulled over and parked. My entire life I heard about Pink's, it was a legendary spot in Los Angeles. I got out of the car and got in line.

"That's a nice hat there, Partner."

"Thanks, it helps hide my massive head trauma."

"Oh, ha, yeah."

The man ahead of me faced forward and left me alone.

The line was a few hundred feet away from the storefront but I saw a steady stream of customers being churned out of the line, smiling and holding hotdogs.

This is how the food stamp office should be. If it had been, I probably wouldn't be in this mess. I'd probably still be alive.

The menu consisted of celebrity names paired with condiment variations. I decided on the Huell Howser chilidog. I wasn't hungry but it seemed like a simple experience I was always denied.

I opened Ivon Springwater's wallet and found it ripe with $100 bills. I paid for the Huell Howser and left a large tip.

As a visual statement, the chilidog did not look appetizing. I am sure the smell and temperature were attracting factors but not for me. I didn't know what to do with it. I carried it across the street.

"Can you spare some change?"

"Would you like this hotdog?"

In a way, this skinny, grungy man in a puffy vest looked like a hotdog himself.

"Hotdog? I appreciate it but no thanks, I don't eat hotdogs."

"Why not?"

"I don't know. They grind up pig ass and who-knows-what. A line of strange meat."

"If you ask me, the way you put it - I think a hotdog is a beautiful metaphor for life."

"Jeez, I guess you have a funny way of looking at things.

"Funny…" I set the hotdog down. "I guess I do."

I pulled out the stolen wallet and handed it to the hotdog looking man and turned to leave.

"Hey wait," he begged. "Take these."

He was offering a pack of cigarettes. A lighter depressed the side of the softpack, wedged between the cardboard and the cellophane wrapping. He tossed it to me.

"Why?" I asked.

"You gave me everything. I'll give you everything," I held the cigarettes up.

"Everything doesn't add up to much for either of us."

"Never does," he replied.

"Now - that's funny."

28.

It was a miracle that The Frolic Room on Hollywood
Boulevard was still open. Hollywood itself was
essentially scorched Earth. The neon sign out front
was the only thing alive for miles.

I stepped in and order a beer.

"I'll start a tab."

I wandered towards the back of the room and took a
seat at one of the red leather stools. I swiveled around
and stared at a mural. I was looking at Laurel &
Hardy and over there were The Marx Brothers.

The television above was silently broadcasting a
Lakers game. They were down by a lot.

On the table next to me was a round black flower,
resting in an empty Corona bottle. Maybe it was
because every time I took a sip of beer flies flew out
of my collar, but the flower's many round, curled,
petals reminded me of a fly's compound eye.

I looked around. Other than the bartender there was
only one other person besides me and he looked
asleep.
The Laker game was interrupted by a news broadcast,
it showed a blurry, black and white clip of me
attaching Linn Ochoco to the subway. It zoomed in
on a clip of me macing her friends. It was too
pixelated to identify me but it was clear – the jig was
almost up.

I took the list out of my breast pocket and crossed off
another name.

~~Parents~~
Eugene Page
Clinton Taggart
~~Linn Ochoco~~
Pershing Haig
Raymond Mitchell-Steele
Schiller Liebe
Henry "Duke" Clayborne
Umatilla Harney
Alberta Wygant

From a basketball standpoint I was shooting 20% from the field. I had killed others but I couldn't just add their names to the list to boost my stats.

"Jesus."

It seemed very unlikely this was going to work out.

I circled the name at the bottom – Alberta. If there was anyone on this list who deserved to go to Heaven it was her.

And I was going to make sure of it.

29.

"This is Lifeline, my name is Jerry. I am here for you."

"Hey Jerry, this is Detective Trenton Ankeny with the Los Angeles Police Department. I need you to transfer me to Kevin."

"Excuse me?"

"I think you heard me perfectly clear Jerry. I know you guys aren't too keen on transferring phone calls, but I don't know Kevin's direct line. So be a dear…"

"A deer?"

"and connect me, goddammit." I finished.

"One second."

"This is Lifeline, my name is Kevin. I am here for you."

"Hey Kevin, this is Detective Trenton Ankeny, of the Los Angeles Police Department, I am following up about those phone calls."

"I beg your pardon, I don't know what you are talking about."

"Don't play coy with me Kevin. I don't have the time for it."

"I'm not playing coy, Sir. I honestly don't know what is going on."

"I called about a few days ago. About a couple of phone calls potentially related to a murder."

"That doesn't ring any bells."

"I don't give a damn about any bells, Kevin. Listen: give me the address of your station. It sounds like I'll have to take care of this myself."

"I don't think I can give out the address over the phone."

"What did I say about being coy, Kevin? Are you testing me? You don't think a fucking police officer can find your office without your help? I have the right mind to come find you after I dig up these files. I might shove them up your ass!"

"Hold on a minute please."

"No, no hold-on-a-minutes, Kevin. Give me the fucking address."

"Okay, are you ready? It is 324 South Broadway. 90013."

I took it down.

"See, Kevin. That wasn't so hard. Now, do me one more favor. Tell your boss I'm coming down there and I'm bringing a warrant to search every goddamn inch of the place, you got it?"

"Yes Sir."

"Another thing. Tell him work is done for the day. Everyone is going home. Got it?"

"Yes Sir."

"That means you. If I catch you in there I'm going to break your ass Kevin."

I hung up.

30.

I hid in the shadows across the street, under the awning of what used to be Grand Central Market. I hunched over my knees and picked at Umatilla Harney's old shoes.

A real chicken drumstick of a man walked out. It was a wonder he didn't topple over his thin legs. I figured that to be Kevin. He moved like a hovering light bulb.

One by one a stream of loafish men exited the building. These were the people in charge of saving lives? The representatives that prove life's worth living?

I almost didn't notice her at first. She was small and lumpy, bundled inside a bubbly coat. Her dark skin nearly the same black as her jacket. She looked like the silhouette of grapes.

She head west, towards the sunset. She carried a large milk crate full of papers. I followed behind her for some time. I had to be sure…

"Alberta?"

She turned and smiled.

"Can I help you?"

"I was actually going to ask you the same thing," I reached for the milk crate.

"No thanks," she cringed away. "Do I know you?"

"In a way, you've helped me many times but we have never officially met," I extended my hand. "My name is Trenton."

"Trenton?" Alberta's voice went up an octave on my second syllable.

"Yes, Alberta. I didn't know if that was you, but somehow, I knew it was."

She looked tired. Physically, emotionally, and mentally.

"Trenton, are you following me?"

"No, Alberta, I don't know how to explain it. I was walking by, I live, well, I used to live just up the street."

"Well, that's fine Trenton. I am glad you are well and it was a pleasure to meet you but I must be going."

"Thanks, but here," I grabbed at the milk crate. "Let me lighten your load, I don't have anything better to do, anyway, I owe you."

"Trenton, you don't owe me anything. In any case I can manage," she tussled with the milk crate but I had a firm grip on it.

"Nonsense."

"Trenton. Give me back my papers."

"Alberta, you are being irrational."

"Trenton, don't you dare comment on my psychological state, especially when it is you who is clearly disregarding the reality of the situation. I don't want you to carry my papers, now, set them down. You are making a very poor first impression."

I threw her crate down and folders and their subsequent papers erupted out of it. She was right. This was a very poor impression. In a way I knew that was a shameful thing but I didn't feel shame. I stormed off.

But, not too far.

When Alberta turned her back to pick up her papers, I returned to the shadows. She looked a lot older than I thought she would. I couldn't tell if it was actual age or the look of age from years at a stressful job. A year at a job like hers was like three years any place else.

She was either suspicious or she felt my presence. I figured it was a combination of the two. For every few blocks she would turn over her shoulder and squint into the night.

But, she never saw me.

Alberta lived on the top row of a tenement in Westlake. Despite the look of her blackberry bubble frame, she moved swiftly the entire journey, never slowing because of the crate, not even when traveling upstairs. She walked across the catwalk and began fiddling with the door to unit 915.

After a few minutes, I withdrew the gun and walked up the remaining flights of stairs.

I peered into the window and saw Alberta was smelling something. I stood on my tippy-toes to see what it was, she was wafting waves of aroma that came smoking out of a crockpot on her counter.

The heat of the smell exited her screen window. How I wished I could share that moment with her.

When she left the kitchen, I put away the gun and tried the door. It was locked. I kicked in the screen and tumbled into the kitchen, taking a series of pots and pans down with me.

Alberta came to investigate, but before she could vocalize her displeasure with the situation, I grabbed her by the throat.

We wrestled; falling on top of her only helped me squeeze the oxygen from her body. Her strength both physical and willpower showed. Alberta Wygant loved life.

"I am sorry Alberta. If you knew why I was doing this, you would thank me for it."

She was limp.

I kissed her on the forehead and got to my feet. She deserved better than this.

I staggered to the next room. Alberta's papers were spread across a giant wood desk. They were case files and a stack of obituaries. I looked through them.

Some of the logs weren't under her name. I saw some names of people I recognized. From the looks of it, Kevin wasn't very good at keeping his callers alive.

Alberta was keeping her own list. It was very similar to mine, but we had completely different views on how to save a soul.

I heard a noise in the kitchen. When I returned I saw Alberta was using the counter to get to her feet.

"No!" I cried.

I ran over to her, plowing her head into the counter. I picked up the crockpot and drove it down onto her heard. The lid flew off from the contact and boiling how stew covered her face.

Alberta's blood curdling howl shook my soul. I backed away in horror.

"No! No!" I couldn't think of anything else more appropriate to say. "No!"

She clawed at the linoleum helplessly. I had to do something. I tripped over her and got to the sink. I put the water on cold and used the hose attachment to rinse the molten meat juice off her skin.

"Stop!" she begged. "What are you doing?"

"I am sorry, I am so sorry."

I pulled the taser out and gave Alberta a shock. The water from the hose acted as a conductor, encapsulating Alberta in a bright bolt of blue energy. The blast circled back around into the taser and caused the device to explode in my hand.

I surveyed the damage. Alberta looked dead and I was missing the top halves of my fingers on my left hand. I bent over and tried to test her pulse but I couldn't feel anything.

"Alberta," I shook her.

She responded with coughing and convulsions.

"Fuck! Alberta, I am so sorry," I said again.

She didn't deserve this. I pulled the gun out of my pants and open fired into Alberta at point blank range. Her head completely spilled open after the fourth bullet but I kept firing anyway. I had to make sure she died.

She had to be. There wasn't much left of her. I set the oven on high and jammed the rest of her inside. I couldn't get her legs in but it was good enough. The heat was sure to finish her off.

I reeled out of the kitchen and struggled with the door. The weight of my actions dazed me.

I flung open the door to a world of sirens. Their wailing screech surrounded me, pummeling me in a Venn diagram of audio waves, representing the intersection of trouble and circumstance.

The lights were close behind, bathing the tenement building in flashes of blue and red. I tried for the stairs but it was no use. There were already policemen ascending them, guns drawn.

I ran across the catwalk but it ended without exit. I had nowhere to go. Except down. I hurtled myself over the railing of the tenement building and soared eight floors to the cold hard cement. Of course I couldn't feel that the cement was cold or hard, but I knew it was. The same way I knew the fall hurt, but I couldn't feel that either.

"Freeze!"

I didn't willingly obey, but I couldn't seem to move much. My body was broken – more than usual. Shortly after that I was at the bottom of a police pig pile.

31.

Jail wasn't so bad.

I couldn't feel anything so I wasn't afraid of anything, which was a good thing because my left arm was clearly broken and I was surrounded by some sketchy people.

"You got anything for me, pussy?"

Some tattoo-faced man stepped across the cell and tried to intimidate me. I pulled my broken arm with my one functioning arm and twisted it into itself, filling the cell with the sounds of pops and cracks.

The tough guy's knees buckled and threw up.

"Aww, fuck!" cried the man nearest the vomit.

"Quiet down in there," the guard grated his baton across the bars.

I looked at the rest of my body and realized my left hip was shattered. My left leg hinged out instead of straight back like it was supposed to look. I struggled to my feet, without feeling I had no balance and without symmetrical limbs I had to put a lot more effort into travelling without falling over.

I did a few laps around the cell, much to the dismay of my fellow cellmates.

"Fuck! Knock it off!"

"I can't take anymore of that cracking."

The tattoo-faced man from earlier was rolled into the fetal position under a bench, dry gagging.

"Stop it! You're going to make me sick!"

"Quiet down in there!" the guard was back.

"You gotta make him stop, Officer!"

"Make him stop!"

A few more policemen came to investigate the commotion.

"What's all the hub-bub?" a larger officer scowled into the cell. "Stop making trouble Ankeny, you hear?"

I ignored them all and practiced my walking.

"Boss, make him stop! He sounds like a fucking bag of teeth."

"Ankeny! You sit down or you'll be sorry."

I caught his eyes.

"Sorry? I doubt it."

"Goddamn it, don't you fucking test me."

I looked at him through the bars and smiled.

"What are you going to do about it you big dumb faggot?"

Despite their previously revulsion towards me, most of the men broke into laughter. I was never one to use homophobic remarks but I wanted to taunt the policeman.

It worked.

"I need back-up at the lockup tank, immediately, repeat, all hands on deck," the cop took his finger of his walkie-talkie; he was now directing his words towards me. "You want me in there with you big boy, you got it."

I turned to my cellmates.

"You guys ready to get the Hell out of here?"

None of them responded. Instead they stared at me with their mouths slack. I pointed at the tattoo-faced man.

"Get him up," no one moved. "Now!"

Two men got to their knees and roused the tattoo-faced man.

"If you see a gun, fucking grab it, got it?"

The men looked at each other. They didn't look like they were enjoying what they were hearing.

A horde of policemen lined up outside the cell. The one with the keys simply opened the door and cleared out of the way, the rest of the line filled the cell.

They prodded me with tasers but the current did nothing to my dead nerves.

However, the sheer force of them was debilitating. A cop with a riot shield smashed me up against the wall.

The police lumped me a few times with their batons and I pretended to go limp. That didn't stop a few of them from getting a few extra licks in.

"Pick him up."

Two officers sandwiched me and pulled me to my
feet. They struggled to get me out of the cell; my
weight was too much for the two of them. They tried
to readjust their grip on me, giving me the perfect
window to attack.
With my right hand free I pulled the revolver free
from the first cops holster. The second cop clapped
his hands over the gun to take control of it but it only
helped line up the perfect shot. I blew his face off.

The first cop fell backwards, shielding himself from
the potential bullets by wildly waving his arms in
front of his face. They did little to actually stop the
bullets though. I pumped him full of lead.

The other officers drew their pistols. They
surrounded me.

"Put it down!"

I didn't listen and with that, all of us opened fire.
Unfortunately, for everyone in the room, I was the
only one who wasn't allergic to bullets.

Most of the cops gunned themselves down, shooting
their partners through me. The ones who survived, I
quickly finished off.

Most of the convicts were dead. The tattoo-faced man
was sitting in a puddle of blood, rocking back and
forth.

I bent over, putting my face in front of his.

"What did you ask me earlier?"

The only thing his face said were the various gang related slogans that were written across it, his mouth moved but no words came out.

"What's that?" I asked.

He was replying but I couldn't hear it.

"I believe you asked if I had anything for you."

I put the gun under his nose – let him smell the death on it. He closed his eyes and shielded his face.

I pushed the gun into his palm. He opened his eyes, and saw I was handing it to him. He refused it initially, then grabbed it and pointed it back at me defensively.

I patted him on the head. I motioned my arms towards the exit and the various dead men that littered the way to it.

"Someday, this could all be yours."

32.

The bus station didn't have much seating but that didn't stop most of people from sitting on their asses – they just did it on the ground. I weaved through talking couples and stepped over sleeping men until I found an open space wide enough for me.

The lighting was very poor in here and the lack of windows only made it worse. Only a few people were under lights, the rest of us waited in the shadows.

I took my fingernail and dipped it in the blood I was covered in and crossed out another name from my list.

~~Parents~~
Eugene Page
Clinton Taggart
~~Linn Ochoco~~
Pershing Haig
Raymond Mitchell-Steele
Schiller Liebe
Henry "Duke" Clayborne
Umatilla Harney
~~Alberta Wygant~~

Despite the fiasco at the police station, I seemed to be gaining momentum.

I tried to count the number of men and women I killed but after a few powers of ten I lost track of how many times I reset my fingers/stubs. It didn't matter what the number was – it was a lot.

In a few hours I hoped to add Clinton Taggart to the growing body count.

Sure, Eugene Page, was the closest person on my list and he was at the top of it too, but the thought of Sherman Caruthers and his robot army – I wanted nothing to do with it.

So I picked the next in line.

Taggart's School for Future Heroes was located outside of Escondido, California. A bit over one hundred miles from Los Angeles. About a four hour bus ride.

I looked at my ticket and back up at the clock. It was getting close to boarding time. However, the glass door exiting to my terminal was still closed.

Since everyone sat where they could, there was no queue or order. Was anyone else waiting for my same bus?

As the clock got closer and closer to the time I got to my feet. Something wasn't right.

"Excuse me? Which bus are you waiting for?"

"Huh?"

"I pointed up at the numbers above the doors."

"Which one are you waiting for?"

"I'm not waitin' for anything. I am resting. Leave me alone."

"Excuse me? Are any of you taking the bus?"

The floor was littered with people staring at me but none of them responded.

"Are you guys resting or waiting?"

"They're the same thing!"

"Yeah! Fuck you!"

I looked at the clock. It was boarding time. I dashed to the glass door to see a queue of people outside, boarding the bus. I clawed at the door but it didn't have a handle on my side.

"Hey!"

I banged on the glass. It caught the attention of the people in line but none of them seemed to care.

"The door is locked!"

I pointed down frantically. Then I pointed at myself and then at the bus. No one seemed to get it, or if they did they weren't going to give up their spot in line to do anything about it.

"Hey!"

"Shut the fuck up!"

"Yeah, be quiet!"

The pleas were coming from behind me, inside the station. I turned around. Everyone on the ground was watching me struggle with the door.

"The quicker you get me out of here the quicker it'll be quiet."

No one moved. I looked back out the glass; the queue was almost entirely boarded. I threw myself at the glass and ricocheted down to the tile floor.

This got quite a reaction from the lazy observers inside the station. They laughed and laughed.

I sprung back up and pounded on the glass like a mad chimpanzee in a zoo. Right as my fist struck the glass, the Bus Driver was walking by to board his bus. The smack on the door startled the Bus Driver and he tripped over and out of sight.

When he returned upright and to my vision I saw he wore a furious scowl, the kind you'd permanently jag into the face of a pumpkin. He flung the glass door open and grabbed me by the throat and pulled me outside.

"What's the big idea?"

"I'm sorry. I was trying to get somebody's attention."

"Congratu-fucking-lations," he tossed me towards the bus. "It worked."

"Thank you."

I stuck my ticket up gently, so he could inspect it but he grabbed it and slapped me over the head with it.

"Get on already."

I don't know if I tripped up the steps or if he kicked me in the ass but I rolled into the bus. I dusted myself off and limped down the walkway.

There were four seats to a row, which was divided by the aisle. Each pair of eyes in each pair of seats studied me until I returned their eye contact, then their eyes pretended they were looking at something else.

The only free seat was at the very back of the bus –
right across from the toilet. I couldn't smell anything
so I didn't see any cons, only the pro of sitting alone.

A toilet on a bus seemed like a cruel joke. Obviously
the Bus Driver can't pull over each time someone on
board has to relieve themself, but was keeping it in a
little bowl in the back of the bus a better solution?

After the Bus Driver finished his rules (the tirade
mostly consisted of various ways to tell us to keep
our mouths shut) he started and we drove into the
sunset.

My window unfortunately faced east. Up ahead I saw
that we were driving alongside the ocean. Everyone
on board had a view of it except me. I could only see
the door to the bathroom. Instead, the view out my
window was a series of browns and greys, subtly
morphing into the blues and blacks of night.

All of the whispers on board found their way into my
ear, hurtling backwards because of the bus's impetus.
I learned many things about my fellow riders, none of
them positive. Everyone was running from something
or somebody.

In a way I was too.

I was running away from Sherman Caruthers. There
isn't a doubt in my mind that if he were in my
position he'd come at me headfirst. Sherman
Caruthers was a fighter. That is why I was afraid of
him.

Clinton Taggart was certainly a fighter in his own
right. In his prime he would certainly be someone to
fear. However, he was old now and most importantly,
he didn't have a wall of robots.

"Pit stop! You have fifteen minutes to do whatever you want. But, in fifteen minutes I am leaving, with or without you."

Before anybody could complain about it, the Bus Driver was already outside with a cigarette hanging from his lips.

I had to wait until all the other passengers made the slow waddle off the bus. By the time I touched the ground we had about ten minutes left.

"Hey, Chief, you got a light?"

"Me? No I'm sorry I don't…" I remembered my trade with the hotdog shaped man. "Actually, I do."

I pulled the dented softpack from my pocket. I saw a bullet had gone through but a good deal of the cigarettes seemed fine. I took the lighter out of the cellophane and preceded to light the various cigarettes before me. As I carried the light from person, they would cup their hands over the flame. The lighter would illuminate their faces.

Everyone was as hideous as me.

I removed an undamaged cigarette from my pack and lit one myself. I had never smoked a cigarette before, and I suppose technically I still hadn't, on account of my lungs and all, but I still enjoyed the experience without the sensations.

For thousands of years, humans gathered around the fire, it was how communities were born. I could see now that smoking cigarettes was a distant relative to the campfire.

We stood in a silent semicircle. Occasionally people shared short stories of where they were going, but they were very short. After all, cigarettes don't last as long as campfires. The flames are not bright enough.

"All aboard!"

I dropped my cigarette out and smashed at the red bits with my heel. Then I moped back to the bus.

33.

All the lights were off in Escondido.

It wasn't late enough for people to be asleep and it was too dark outside to not use lights. Clearly, there was nobody around.

I walked in the darkness for a short time, and then I lit another cigarette, allowing the burning tobacco in my lips to light my way.

A sign above the main strip of town declared this street Grand Central Avenue and much like both Grand and Central in Los Angeles, this street was coated in sleeping homeless.

The wet grass hid the sounds of my footsteps. I was trying to be respectful of the sleepers. It was a lot quieter here than it was in Skid Row.

It didn't seem to matter; I saw plenty of rolling eyes follow me down the road. I was like a video camera at a baseball game, panning along with 'the wave' as it spirits through the stadium.

No matter where I turned there were people in the streets, both awake and asleep. Small huddles of men clumped around flaming trashcans - another distant cousin of campfires.

I was half way across town before I saw any real lights. A few windows in the upper floors of homes had them. A neon blinking sign outside of a bar read: COCKTAILS. A gas station had lights on both their signs and pumps. Everything else in the city was dark until a car drove by.

Taggart's School for Future Heroes was a few miles west on the outskirts of town. It occupied a former college campus, allowing them to utilize existing classrooms.

It was clear which buildings were dormitory residence and which were classrooms because of the lights. Most of the campus lay in darkness. But the two dormitory towers on campus were visible for miles down the road.

Other than the moon and the stars they were the only lights in the sky.

Mission Road ended before the campus. A giant security gate blocked my path. I approached anyway.

"Halt! Who goes there?"

I couldn't see who was asking, I could only see their flashlight pointing at me. I shielded myself.

"It is Trenton Ankeny."

"Ankeny?"

"Yeah!"

The flashlight redirected from my face to the dirt in front of me. I took a few steps but the flashlight was back in my face.

"Halt! I don't see your name on our list."

"There must be some sort of mistake. I am here to see Clinton Taggart."

"Yes, then there is a mistake. Mr. Taggart is in New York on business."

Without a word I turned back around and walked back into Escondido.

The way back was darker. The dormitories had irradiated the journey to the school but the way back east had nothing. Only darkness.

"What a waste of time." I muttered.

"Shhhh."

I didn't see who hushed me but I heard them all the same. A few times I had to step over the bodies that littered the roads, they blended into the darkness. I tripped over a few and they voiced their displeasure about it.

I turned back onto a familiar street and walked straight for the buzzing neon cocktail sign. The maneuver was more moth-like than alcoholic.

The inside of the bar was too bright. Dozens of televisions lined the room. A jukebox drowned out all of their audio with accordion. It took my eyes a second to adjust from being out in the darkness for so long, but then I found a seat by the bar.

I stuck my hand in the air "Can I have a beer?"

"Let's see some ID."

"I'm old enough to drink I assure you."

"I can see that. I ain't never seen you in here before, I don't know you, so I want to see some ID."

"Listen…"

"No, you listen, this is my bar and I got a bad feeling about you. Now cough up some ID or get the fuck out.

"Who's that Cheeser?" barked a voice from the back.

"Aw, shut up!" I replied.

"That's it! Get the fuck out of my bar!"

I did as he asked. I walked toward the exit, defeated. I hated Escondido.

"Hey! Hey, wait a minute!"

I kept walking.

"Cheeser! Grab him!"

I turned to see what was going on.

"It *is* him!"

"It's the vagina killer!"

"Vagina killer?" I laughed.

But, it wasn't funny for long. These men meant business. Two biker's thundered through cocktail tables and chairs, plowing straight for me.

"I knew I recognized you from somewhere!"

The one called Cheeser revealed a shotgun hidden under the bar.

They were coming at me.

Buckshot flew out the door along with me. I ran a few steps and looked back to see if they were still chasing me.

They were.

"Stop him!"

"Grab him! He's a murderer!"

The shouting roused some men on the sidewalks. Their eyes found me quickly.

I hobbled by as fast as I could, but the two bikers were hot on my heels.

The sound of whispering grew louder as news spread through the homeless. Those who had heard of my crimes sat up, they wanted to see. A few pointed at me.

"Vagina vagina vagina vagina," I heard the whisper follow me. The words were faster than me.

So were the bikers.

My body was too wrecked. - my spine, my hip, my legs. I couldn't run properly.

I turned down the next street. My drastic entrance caught the eyes of the men surrounding the trashfires. The flames danced in their wet eyes.

"Grab him!"

"Stop him!"

"That man is a murderer."

Unlike the previous homeless who were sleeping or simply pretending to be asleep - the homeless on this street were standing. They were warm. They were angry.

They were ready, willing and able.

A flock of men peeled away from the trashfires. Others grabbed sticks and wood debris, dipping it into the fire to create torches. They were all coming straight for me.

"Please stop!" I yelled.

The walls were closing in. Furious men and women ran at me from both sides. I ran for my only exit – a dark alley.

"Stop him!"

Someone hiding in the darkness of the alley grabbed my legs but I shook free and continued my escape.

Up ahead was a parking lot. I saw a woman walking toward a pick up truck, keys in hand.

"Stop him!"

She turned to see what the commotion was but I had already swung. Her face spun into my fist and then her head careened off the sidewalk. I yanked the keys from her hand and fiddled with the door.

I got in and locked the doors behind me. They were nearly upon me. I couldn't see the ignition in the darkness so I jabbed the key around until it stuck, but when I turned them they dropped to the ground.

"Fuck you murderer!"

"Get him!"

The crowd had caught up. They surrounded the vehicle. Men with torches filled the air with light. I could see all the hatred in their glowing faces.

I scrabbled the floor for the keys.

"Got it!" I yelled.

Before I could try for the ignition again, a fist came through the window. It retreated quickly in pain but that only made room for more arms to enter the vehicle. Some tried for the door. Others tried for me. The big biker from the nameless bar grabbed a chunk of my face.

The keys found their home. I gave it a turn and the engine roared to life.

"Get him!"

I slammed on the gas and the audience in front of my windshield disappeared.

The biker was still hanging in the window, his fingers taut on my loose face skin. I accelerated and it was too much for the biker's feet to manage. He fell out the window, most of my face still in his hand.

I looked in the rearview mirror and saw there were a few cars pulling out on the road behind me.

Then I saw my skull smiling at me in the mirror.

I smashed the gas pedal as far down as it could go but the truck lumbered heavily.

I thought I heard gunshots.

The rearwindow burst into the cab, hundreds of glass shards went down my shirt collar and onto my lap.

I did hear gunshots.

My vehicle was too slow. A red sedan was already on my ass, attempting to bump me into a fishtail. But, luckily my truck was heavier than the sedan. The other sets of headlights were closing the gap.

The twin dormitory towers glowed in the night like beacons.

More gunshots.

I looked at the dashboard. I was only going 55 MPH. A red light was blinking at me. I squinted and read the tiny words: "emergency brake".

I looked over and saw the brake bulging upwards like an erection. I released it and the truck ripped forward. The speedometer climbed higher and higher.

I looked up and saw the security gate of Taggart's School. I didn't have time to react. I plowed through the fence and spilled onto campus.

My rearview showed a half dozen cars and trucks were still hot in pursuit.

My new speed was too much to handle. I overcorrected a turn and lost control of the truck, skidding off the road and barreling right into a domed building.

I forgot my seatbelt.

I exited the vehicle through the windshield, which was actually convenient. I got to my feet and ran for the door of the building. It was unlocked.

This was an observatory. Through the doors was a giant amphitheater. In the center of the room hung a series of metallic balls. I removed the velvet rope off a pair of stanchions and pulled both of them to the door. I put the first one through the handles. Then I levered the base of the other under the door.

"Get him!"

"Kill him!"

The chanting outside was growing louder.

They were here.

"Kill him!"

I grabbed both doors and propped my legs under the stanchion. I pulled as hard as I could.

But, then I heard - they weren't trying to open the door. They were trying to block it.

"What's going on?"

I spun around and saw a handful of dirty white-faced children in white uniforms. As a group they looked like popcorn.

"There are some crazy people outside. We need to find another exit."

"Who is crazy?"

"That's the only way out."

"Shut up!"

I swiped at the kids and they popped back into the hallway dividing the amphitheater.

"Kill him!"

"Kill him!"

I heard banging on the wall next to the door. I got closer and put my ear up to the wall, but all I could hear was the crowd's refrain.

"Kill him!"

"Kill him!"

The banging was louder now. It was something metal. But, I couldn't place it.

Had I a sense of touch or a sense of smell I could have probably picked up on things a bit sooner. It wasn't until fire tickled up the back of the doors that I realized what was going on.

I backed into the amphitheater.

The popcorn kids bunched by the far wall, a series of lights sprayed out of the various-sized metal balls. They covered the boys in a map of the stars.

"What's going on Mister?"

"Boys, we have to call for help."

"What happened to your face?"

"It doesn't matter. Listen: the people outside set the building on fire."

"Fire?" they said in unison. I heard more curiosity than fear in their voices.

"Where is the phone?"

"There is no phone Mister."

"Why did they set the building on fire?"

"There isn't a lot of time to explain it boys. We need to figure out a way out of here."

"Do they hate science? Mr. Taggart says some people hate science."

"I don't know boys. Some people do evil things."

"Mr. Taggart says to be a hero we have to fight evil."

"You don't understand…"

"Mr. Taggart says the only thing to fear is fear itself."

"Stop! One, Mr. Taggart didn't come up with that…" I tried.

"Mr. Taggart says it doesn't matter who is first it matters who does it right."

"Stop!" I didn't want to hear what Mr. Taggart said.

I wanted out.

I head back towards the exit. The fire was through the door, reaching its long hot hands towards me. The dense smoke collecting on the ceiling started to glow too, it was backlit by more fire.

"There has to be another way."

I went back into the amphitheater. I stared at the ceiling, there had to be a way out.

"What about up there?"

I pointed to the roof.

"Huh?"

"Boys, we gotta get out of here! Is there a way onto the roof?"

The stars on their faces washed away into darkness. The power was out. The room was pitch black.

"Boys?" I yelled. "Can you hear me?"

"It's going to be okay Mister."

A pulsing light danced into the amphitheater. It was the fire. It was spreading fast.

"I can be a hero.
You can be a hero.
Everyday we can try... "

"Stop singing! You kids don't seem to understand what is going on here."

"Hey Mister, don't be afraid."

The boys resumed their singing. I stood there facing the darkness.

"I can be a hero.
You can be a hero.
Everyday we can try.
But, you can't live with fear-oh
Be afraid of zero.
Because you can't be a hero until you try. "

As dumb as the song was, it was getting to me. Not the lyrics, but the fact the boys sang.

Sang in the face of danger.

The fire seized the carpet and traced right into the amphitheater. The dancing lights reflected off the glass and metal surfaces of the balls that hung in the center of the room.

Stars of fire filled the air.

I could see the boys, huddled together, holding hands. The sound of the fire raged over their voices but from their identical mouth movements I could tell they were still singing.

I stared at those boys with envy. So young and so brave. They were braver than I ever was or ever will be. Dead or alive.

The smoke got to them before the fire did. I saw them coughing.

It was over.

The boys formed a circle and hugged.

It was over for me. It was over for me a long time ago.

But, it wasn't over for these boys.

I thought of all the things in my life I never did. Each unaccomplishment added a tear in the fabric of my soul.

These boys had so much life to live. So many mistakes to make. So many things to learn.

I couldn't stand by and watch them die.

Heaven can wait.

I ran to the far wall and pulled the fire extinguisher off of it. I lumbered it across the burning floor and up to the boys.

I added my face to the center of the boys huddle. I yelled over the fire and into their ears.

"Boys! Listen. I am going to open the doors. Once you see them open I need you to get out of here okay. You can be heroes today. I know you can."

"Mr. Taggart says to be a hero we have to fight evil."

I handed that boy the fire extinguisher and nodded.

"Mr. Taggart was right," I told him.

Rule Number Two: don't turn your back on evil – conquer it.

The fire ate my clothes except for the polyester pants; they melted into a hard plastic, which shattered as I trudged forward into the heat.

My hands melted onto the red hot metal of the first stanchion. I pulled it free and most of my skin went with it.

The stanchion wedged under the door was trickier. The heat had welded the metal into the doorframe. I grabbed the first stanchion and brought it down as hard as I could on the pedestal, and again, and again.

I burst into flames.

But, I didn't stop smashing. I continued to use the first stanchion as a sledgehammer on the wedged stanchion.

I felt something.

I felt something!

I felt... itchy!

Finally, the melted pedestal broke and the door was free.

From my side at least.

The door banged on something outside of reach.

I felt so itchy. I scratched my neck and a sloop of molten skin dripped off my bones.

I felt hot.

This was it. I had one last shot. I took a few bounds backward and clapped.

My hands were nothing but bone and boiling sinew.

"Get ready boys!"

My melted feet provided great traction. I ran forward, striking with everything I have.

My life was over.

"God, please. If I do anything. Let it be this."

I braced my arm and plunged into the door with everything I would, should, or could have.

34.

"Would you kids shut the fuck up?" yelled the man across from me.

"What?" I gasped.

It took me a few seconds to process where I was.

"I wasn't talking to you, assho…"

The man was intending on facing me when he said: "asshole" - for emphasis. Instead, he saw what I looked like and stuttered the rest.

"lelelele. I, uh…"

He turned back around, I tried to grab his shoulder but I no longer had a hand. I had a charred stump.

I was dead.

"Don't touch me!" he screamed.

"Would you quiet down?" The lady behind him had had enough.

"Yeah, okay," he settled down.

"Shhhh."

I peaked behind me and the line seemed to grow and grow. My eyes couldn't comprehend it. It was like trying to draw a pen through a maze with your eyes crossed.

"Sir, please stop looking this way."

"Yeah, Jesus Christ. Have some common courtesy."

I obliged.

There was a lot of space between the next person and me. It wasn't until we all took a step forward that I saw there were piles.

They seemed to scoot forward too.

"Boys?"

"Oh, hey Mister."

"Look it's that guy from earlier."

"You can see me?"

"Yeah," they said in unison. "Why?"

"Oh. Um, no reason."

The others around me gritted their teeth in smiles of pity.
"Where are we?"

"We're in Heaven, boys. We made it."

I still had no concept of time but when the piles of ash sang their song for the thousandth time, I started using that as a constant.

When I reached the front – I had been in line for 140,611 verses. I didn't know how that converted into minutes but I knew it was a long time.

All five piles scooted off together to be judged. It didn't seem like it took long. They scooted away into Heaven.

I was next.

"Well, if it isn't the man of the hour! Trenton Ankeny."

"You know who I am?"

"Oh, you fucking bet I do! I made a killing off you today."

"Glad I could help."

"Oh, you don't even know. I'm going to be a new man up here thanks to you."

"Good for you."

"I just want you to know I mean that. I truly do. That's why I am going to try to put this, well; I didn't actually expect you'd be in my line. I can't believe it," he was blushing.

I tried to smile at him but I didn't have any lips so technically I already was.

"First off, I just wanted to give you some good news. Your friend, well," he snorted when he laughed. "Not your friend, per se, but Alberta. Alberta Wygant. I wanted to let you know she made it in."

"Great, I really owe her an apology..."

"Well, uh, that's where the bad news comes in."

"What bad news?"

He motioned his arms, they said: "take a look around."

"The only bad news there is up here, Trenton. But, I want you to know that those boys you tried to save.

They made it in. They were some of the last souls to make it."

"So what's the bad news?"

"Are you still lost Trenton? I'm trying to tell you - you're aren't coming in again."

"Is it because I killed people?"

He started laughing hysterically. When he calmed down he let me know – yes.

"Yeah, let's just say you went a little overboard back there, Trenton."

He motioned which door was for me. I looked at him and looked back at the door.

"Goodbye," I said and walked towards my destiny.

"Wait, Trenton."

I stopped.

"One more thing."

"What?"

"A guy named Loki, he left a message for you. It says: 'ask him if he found out what is funny.' What should I tell him?"

"Everything. Everything is funny."

www.ingramcontent.com/pod-product-compliance
Lightning Source LLC
Chambersburg PA
CBHW020729210626
46807CB00016B/531